The Fifth Journal

The Fifth Journal

Book One of the Sons of Sanhedrin Series

Matt Sims

authorHOUSE®

AuthorHouse™
1663 Liberty Drive
Bloomington, IN 47403
www.authorhouse.com
Phone: 1-800-839-8640

Published by AuthorHouse   05/10/2012

ISBN: 978-1-4685-4693-4 (sc)
ISBN: 978-1-4685-4694-1 (hc)
ISBN: 978-1-4685-4695-8 (e)

Library of Congress Control Number: 2012901341

Any people depicted in stock imagery provided by Thinkstock are models, and such images are being used for illustrative purposes only.
Certain stock imagery © Thinkstock.

This book is printed on acid-free paper.

Because of the dynamic nature of the Internet, any web addresses or links contained in this book may have changed since publication and may no longer be valid. The views expressed in this work are solely those of the author and do not necessarily reflect the views of the publisher, and the publisher hereby disclaims any responsibility for them.

Preface

It fell upon me, naturally by default, to introduce this journal to you and the many others to follow; yet, I found through it all that I cannot write like he could. How could I find it within myself to fake such a responsibility? Nevertheless, I did reach back within the recesses of my mind and found that I still was able to write poetry like I had from so long ago. It is with great pleasure and pride that I share with you the poem I wrote for this book. For it is with the overwhelming emotional stake I have in this family that I am able to bring forth the words that I wrote. My sons gave so much to me and may they never stop giving to those in need.

The mysterious man

Oh what have you done?

You man of mystery, you man of greed,

You led these men and you made them bleed.

They cry out for a savior and you do not see.

That these men you lead and my everlasting plea,

They go unheard,

They are unseen.

Oh man of mystery man of greed,

Listen to me now and forget the deed,

The one that made me hate you,

The one that made me heed.

For the words I speak and the lessons I have learned,

They were costly,

Yet they were earned.

Oh man of mystery man of greed,

Do not forget the men you lead.

For without them the fight is not true,

And without them there is only you.

Do not steal from them the children they bear,

Or take refuge in the lives they share.

For without them the wicked prevail

and the mighty will perish,

And not one will ever see this legacy they cherish.

Oh man of mystery man of greed,

Please listen to my everlasting plead.

Do not steal innocence from the young,

Or rob wisdom from the old.

For it is the men of neither that remain ever bold,

They stand fast in front of you,

Forever protecting us from the evil of those that do,

I say man of mystery, man of greed,

Lead with a soft tongue and throw away the iron fist.

For if you decide to ignore my word,

And hide from me as if you do not exist,

These men you have led,

The ones sleeping at home in their beds,

They will not falter and they will not coup,

They will simply and fiercely,

Come after you!

Oh man of mystery, man of greed,

Do not take lightly the message in my plea.

For if you do, you will find,

My sons will come after you in due time.

This message I give you,

This message you should keep.

For If they should come,

And I promise you they will,

They will surely find you in your sleep . . .

Introduction

I remember sitting in a class once, the teacher was rambling on about some type of sociological phenomenon or communicational breakthrough, I can't really say because my mind was elsewhere. There was a girl in the classroom that I couldn't stop thinking about. Her hair hung down in waves, and every time she moved her head the hair would dance around her so eloquently. She never seemed to be out of the sunlight; rays would pour down around her, engulfing her in a beautiful grace, indoors or out. Her skin was olive colored without a blemish upon it, and her modesty was truly visible through the attire she chose to wear. I knew I loved her the moment I saw her, everything about her spoke to me in the simplest of ways. When we locked eyes for the first time it was as if we had always known each other, like we had come home from a long journey apart. The first time I saw her smile it melted me inside; I fell apart and I knew only she could put me back together.

It didn't take long for her to notice my charm and for me to hold her hand. But in a room of sloths and toads, how could she not see me I asked myself. We would stand there, or sit; often on the cliffs that overlooked the ocean near the town we lived in and just enjoy our time together. The months passed and our lives intertwined together, joined by drastic ups and downs. We loved each other during that time and opened our hearts to one another, sharing the most intimate of secrets. The parts of our lives that no one else was privy to, we were able to see, and the trust laid down between us was something deeper and more profound than I had ever experienced before. Our relationship grew and instead of it being like everything that had come before it, something on the surface or merely mist in the wind, it had become a part of me, an integral piece I felt that I could not survive without.

The day came, however, when our paths adjusted, the alignment was off and something felt mortally wrong. She walked away from me, and there was nothing I could do. She said her love didn't cease, yet our connection did. I replayed the vision of her walking away from me for months, moreover years, after that day. It was the worst day of my life and it caused me the worst possible pain that I had ever experienced. For years to come after that day, I would know nothing else. The sun lost its warmth, the flowers ceased to blossom, and the birds no longer sang. Darkness settled on the plains of my mind; the rolling fields of green died that day and wilted into dust. My path wouldn't be straight for months after that day. I was lost for quite a while, zigzagging back and forth trying to find my way amongst the shadows. It wasn't until I could no longer see her path that I was able to straighten out my own. Her voice was only a whisper in memory, and the vision of her was skewed, replaced with outlines and shapes rather than detail and stark reality.

The part of me that felt alive with her no longer existed, replaced with scar tissue and indistinct concepts of what used to be. I had to start over, fix what was broken, replace what was lost, and create that which needed to be created. I saw my path straighten, my vision clear up, and my future returned. I had meaning once more, perhaps it wasn't the meaning I had desired, but it was a meaning I needed and a drive from which I could not turn. My college years came to an end several months later, and I realigned with my brothers, all of whom were older than I and much farther along in life. Even though I could see the path I needed to take, the amazing monstrosity of the hole she left inside me became a constant distraction and deterrent from taking the first step down a much needed road of recovery.

My oldest brother approached me shortly after I watched her walk away on that dreadful day. He put his arm around me and told me not to forget the things that had happened to me; not to forget the things that had created me and shaped the person I had become; that the person I am today is because of all the things I have endured, good and bad. He told me I needed to use the gifts given to me, that I needed to record our lives; the lessons learned, the sacrifices made, the losses we suffered, and the many more to come. All of this fell upon me to remember. I would forever carry the burden of the past upon my shoulders, and it would be my burden alone. My eyes had always been on the future and would remain so, yet now I was given the responsibility of remembering the past as well. The burden would only be lessened by the thoughts I put down on paper. I began to notice that my stress buildup was alleviated when I wrote. I found great relief in writing, feeling as though waves of freedom were accompanied with every movement of my pen on paper.

I know that stories like this seem to always start with a girl; yet, this one in particular changed the world for me, and I want to share it with you. Perhaps though, this story is not the generic Hollywood venture we are all so used to or that you may be expecting. If you haven't noticed already, happy endings are truly hard to come by in the real world. Often the hero loses and the victor is eventually hated. Nevertheless, it is a good story, one that I am happy to tell and honored to have been witness to and an active part of. I return my focus now to the class I was once sitting in, the teacher is still actively trying to convey his thoughts regarding the topic at hand. Something he says triggers my hearing; I bolt back from unconscious awareness and plug myself once more into the conversation being heard.

He says something I wasn't sure I heard right. So he says it again, this time I hear it and subtly smirk to myself. What a farce man is at times, thinking he is above the animals, that he is somehow better than the creatures of the sea or the birds of the air. To think that the roaming animals of the plains are beneath him is to visualize his every waking thought. To him, he is a god, rising above this world with visions of greatness, not a mere mortal but a breathtaking star of hope and everlasting joy. To him, he is the beginning and the end; yet, only he thinks these things. It is not until he sees the idiocy of his ways, and sees the slander in saying he is more than a mere man, that he is able to truly become who he is and always was meant to be, a servant.

I watch these words pour forth from the instructor's lips, confidence backs them as they flow over the tainted, studious sponges sitting around me. The vomit is quickly absorbed and processed. The process is now beginning to repeat itself, and soon these sponges will spew forth their contents on more sponges. Eventually, the contents will have been changed, skewed ever so slightly and misrepresented forever. The story will be lost, misplaced, and exponentially misused. The gods themselves will look upon each other with reverence and think they have done it again. They will see only their triumphs and diligently forget their faults. I am here, I think to myself; to never let them do so, to forever remind them they are faulty, frail, and mortal.

The instructor's words are now piercing, and I can't get them out of my head. "We are all geniuses in our own right," he says. "Individual genius it is called. We each have gifts that no other individual possesses. Therefore, there are destinies on this planet that only the individual can complete." I smirked and thought, "Really?" Even if this is true, there is no way that the majority can or do fulfill their destinies. I can say without doubt, shame, or hesitation that the masses rarely complete the paths laid out for them. All too often the individual is kept down, chained to a post like a beaten dog. He never rises to his full potential because he has no drive to get there, scarred from a lifetime of pain and disappointment. The quieter, easier path is more often chosen and the weak wander the earth yearning for their death, hoping it will never come, praying every day that it does quickly and swiftly. Those few, however, that realize their potential greatness and spend every waking moment fighting for it—only they can be recognized.

I will recognize them here in the words I have put down on paper; in this journal you are about to read. Some of you may have a personal part in this story, some of you may never have heard anything about this story, but I guarantee all of you will be moved by it. My brothers in arms, my brothers in life, my friends, and my family, all of them that I grew to love and fight for, gave everything they had to make sure I could fulfill my destiny. But the most extraordinary part is that by reading this story, you are fulfilling a part of yours. The individual genius does exist and can be found; it's up to you to find them, become one, and to not give up until you do. Failure preys upon the weak and grips the souls of those that give up before the fight is done. We don't have to win at everything, but we can't give up trying; once we do we have lost it all, and the successful write life's story. I write this with a smile, thinking that if I am writing this story now and you are reading it, we both know who has won, in one way or another . . .

Chapter 1

. . . Life Before . . .

It is funny, I think, looking back at my life after the girl of my dreams walked away. I wonder why it is that there are moments in time one can look back upon with such pent-up frustration or emotion, even though they seem like, or even may be, eons ago. To this day the simple thought of her makes my heart want to blow out of my chest, the pounding within me is almost too much to bear. It's amazing really, that the simplest of things can take us back to the very moments for which we harbor such strong feelings. Sometimes it is as little as a scent in the air, or a song we hear on the radio that instantly teleports us backwards, to a time we most often would rather forget. I had set out defiantly to bury myself in things, hobbies, sports, goals, anything so that I could forget my past and all the heartache that accompanied it. The only problem with this, though temporarily successful, is that you never forget your past. You just learn to hide from it better; in the end though, it always catches up to you.

No matter how fast you run, or how good you get at hiding, you will turn the corner some day at a grocery store, or be stopped at a red light and look over, only to see someone you wished you could have gone without seeing. It's rather comical at times how all the individual paths in this life intertwine eventually; no matter how diligent one is trying to prevent it. Thinking back, I remember trying to date everyone I met just so I could forget her; the only trouble I had with that was almost every girl reminded me of her. The ones that didn't, however, made me only wish they did. I tried really hard for a long time to forget. After a while her scent faded from the air, her voice became a whisper, and her laugh blended with the wind. I found that forgetting her made everything worse, as I lost something that I had created with her. The pain that I had became the only thing that held me together, and trying to get rid of it started to pull me apart at the seams. A year went by and all my attempts at fixing it had failed. I decided then and there I needed a new tactic, something unconventional, and something inexplicitly new. I settled on the idea that instead of ridding myself of her, every memory, every vested emotion, that I should harness it and prove her wrong in some ways, and right in so many others.

She had faith in me and saw my potential in so many exciting outlets. She knew she had to complete her own path on her own, and in doing so would have to let me go. I lost my faith in her when she cut me off. I blamed her for my pain, and I hated her for it for a long time. She left me because she needed to heal herself from the pains of her family prior to meeting me, and that was something I couldn't help her with, or so she said. Once I realized and believed that she left because of circumstances beyond my control, it was only then that I was able to move forward and get beyond my slump. I found the ability to organize my feelings and thoughts into a constructive pattern, which in turn revealed my own potential. However, I moped around for a while, pitying myself and losing sight of what was important, and ultimately sitting on the ideas that could free me from my self-created prison. I was finally able to pull the crap from my eyes when my oldest brother came to me with an idea.

One thing I always liked about my oldest brother Eddie was that his ideas were always solid; they were well thought out and resembled a lot of how our father would think. When my brother proposed ideas, he did so after much thought of his own. He would spend countless days, sometimes weeks, researching and fine-tuning every conceivable perception of the idea before he would even dream of letting any of us in on it. Because of this formula to his plan he never once came forth with a shitty idea. More or less, his ideas were concrete and stable, and would always benefit anyone who involved themselves in them. Many of the ventures he chose to pursue over the years prior to the conflict resulted in a lot of his friends and family benefiting both financially and emotionally. He never made anyone rich, but he certainly did not make any of them poor. His current idea was the result of an inner passion he had kept dormant for so many years; fearful it would be frowned upon. When he came to me I realized that I was the first person he had talked to about this, and if I didn't approve I might be the last person he ever spoke to about it.

It had been almost a year since he approached me on the day she left. He ventured to guess that I had become quite good at writing and had at the very least kept a journal all these months. Being right wasn't something he was unaccustomed to and I smirked back at him when he asked, knowing full well he already knew the answer. I mentioned my journal and the many entries I had made, along with the long overdue need for a change in my life. With that statement of mine he smiled and said he had a proposition for me and the rest of the family, if we wanted in. He started off mentioning only a little, to feel out my reaction to the new idea he had. I was intrigued and a little overwhelmed at the venture, but, nevertheless, I wanted in. I desperately needed a change in my life, to apply meaning to it once again. I know looking back that it is always wise to say that "Nothing lost is nothing gained," but when you are buried under a pile of your own self-pity and remorse it is difficult to see the light even when you are sitting right underneath it. On that day my brother showed me the light and a list of goals I could set for myself. I was in, and I wanted nothing to do with any view in the rear view mirror; there was no looking back.

His idea was simple, prepare for the worst. That was it, there were no tricks, and there were no gimmicks or empty promises. He said it plain and clear, whatever you put into this is what you will get out of it. He wanted to establish a group of people that could rely on each other in anything, friends if you will, until the bitter end. He wanted each of his brothers to have a part in it, all five of us had something to bring to the table, and he wanted each of us to maximize our potential. There were several friends he spoke of that he knew would already be an asset and he envisioned there being many more people who would want to be a part of this. Granted, it might at first sight appear crazy, overly eccentric, and downright nutty, but beyond all the appearance of paranoia lay true wisdom that I am ashamed I overlooked for so long.

Preparing for the worst has become such a stigma in mainstream thought. People often see the guy buying fifty pounds of rice or twenty-five pounds of salt in the store and think, "What in the heck is this guy doing?" Then, some minor catastrophe strikes, an earthquake rattles some nerves, a tornado flips lives upside down, or rain seems to never stop, and panic sets in. People end up rushing the local grocery stores, causing ridiculous riots or killing each other over a sandwich. All of this could have been prevented with a little preparation and sound judgment. My brother had it in his head that with the combined effort of a few, they could provide for many. He turned out to be right yet again, and over the next several years we all pulled together to accomplish quite a bit.

My brothers were easy to convince; in fact, it didn't take convincing for any of them. Most were already doing some small part on their own without anyone else being aware of it. Each of my brothers had pursued a profession in government work in one fashion or another. As cliché as it may appear, they truly were America's heroes. Between the four of them there was the oldest Eddie, a firefighter/paramedic, the second oldest Chaz, a Marine Recon Sniper, the third oldest Dylan, a Police SWAT Officer, and the fourth bother Howard, an Air Force Pararescue soldier. Then, at the end of the line, there was a college graduate and aspiring writer, me. My name is James, and it's no wonder I felt the way I did at one point or another, slightly inadequate and the youngest of five boys. You stand me up next to them and we don't seem any different, all built the same and pretty much the same size, yet once you look at our résumés the differences become all too real. My mother always said that all her sons were just as capable and as brilliant as the other, however, our paths took us all in different directions.

She raised each of us in similar yet different ways. We five were every bit the same as we were different, which left a lot to the uncertain as to how we would all turn out. She mentioned to me once that it was always interesting when we were growing up to see the day we became bigger than she. Her years of discipline came to a grinding halt once the realization that we were now a foot taller than she and far stronger entered our minds. It was then that our father took us aside to have a word. He wanted to instill in us the knowledge of the responsibility that accompanied new attributes like strength and domineering presence. He made sure we realized that we were never to overpower someone or to, at any time, place someone in a position of subservience, unless to protect ourselves or the ones we loved. He wanted us to be servants of others and to constantly and everlastingly give until we could no longer give anymore. He entrusted us with our new abilities and told us that it was now our job to protect our mother just as she had protected us all our lives up to this point.

Now, all the servant-hood stuff aside, my father would be the first person to severely injure or kill someone that ever compromised his or his family's safety. This meant that he wanted us to feel the same way towards family and the importance of maintaining its sound structure. He stressed this to no end because without a family, one is alone, and survival is not a lonely operation. Sure, you may be able to last a little while, but the loneliness alone would drive someone insane. The sheer amount of time it took to maintain a proficient food supply and to guard that food supply would wipe one person out. There would be no time for rest, and in turn mistakes would be made and consequences would be suffered. With this in mind, my father took it upon himself to properly instill that awareness within his sons to never forget that life was to be tackled by a team and not by a lone soldier. My oldest brother took this to heart more than any of us, and he always seemed to carry that burden.

I can recall over the years seeing it truly take its toll on my oldest brother through many aspects, but most of all in his dating life. He never quite seemed to find the right girl or something would come up between them. There seemed to always be something with him, and I feel it had a lot to do with his belief that the outcome of his brothers resulted from his actions, like he was the overall representative of, "How to live one's life" to each of us. I do recall my parents telling him at one time that the younger boys look up to him as a role model, and that they in turn want to do anything and everything he does. I feel that really impacted him; perhaps he thought that one false move he made would in turn result in four other false moves by us, and we would all at once fall over this metaphorical cliff. Because of this, I think he always felt he must wait for that perfect girl that would come along and represent the ideal woman each of us should pursue.

That perfect girl never did come though, and as far back as I can recall, he was never with a girl more than a few weeks. I think this really saddened him at times, making him feel as though he was doing something wrong. Sometimes I think his expectations for what that girl should be like and look like were a tad bit to high; ultimately, the image in his head just never really existed in the real world. He eventually found peace though, and that much was visible in his eyes as he got older. He began to walk more upright and display a confidence that the world envies. He settled into his life and focused all his energy on helping those around him succeed with him, and in turn his rewards were endless. This was why I was so excited to pursue this new venture of his. Besides giving me a new and profound purpose, it was also backed by a man that, to me, had become a beacon of excellence and was the ultimate representation of success. I was proud of my brother, who he was, and who he had become in his life. He was someone you could always count on; by default he was way too reliable and when he said he would be somewhere or do something he never failed to follow through. His word, like the rest of my brothers, had always remained true and was the bond by which they valued their lives. In short, once I stepped onto this bandwagon there was no looking back, I was all in.

This journal of mine was never meant to be an instruction manual or some kind of "how-to" book on preparation, so forgive me for not going into detail about the training we went through. If you really are interested and want to travel down the same path we did, then have at it! There are tons of people out there ready to take your money and feed you a bunch of crap; it is up to you to wade through the bullshit and find the truth buried in it. My job is not to baby anyone, nor will I attempt any efforts to do so or make your path easier than mine was. You want this, you go get it yourself and suffer through it like we did. With that, I will step off my soapbox and get back to what really matters here, our story.

Like previously mentioned, I had been primarily unfocused in my life thus far. Of course, I was able to complete college and hold down a steady job writing for a local newspaper, but anyone can finish college. Just because you are able to take a class and attain a grade means nothing in the realm of responsibility and aspiration. What a grade or degree means is that you are simply able to put up with numerous self-centered professors and their idealistic, empty-headed student teacher aids. A degree means nothing on its own. I am sorry if that pains you to hear, but it's overwhelmingly true. Look at the statistics alone, they are leaning heavily in favor of my statement. How many college grads do you know who have degrees in Biology, Sociology, Math, English, and so on that are working in some restaurant, or an oil change station? The amount is staggering. It's not what degree you have or the major you pursued that defines you anymore, but what you decided to do with your life thereafter.

Due to the mind-numbing amount of pain I still suffered from after my heart was broken, I demanded from myself that I not let it ever happen again. A little over a year after she turned her back on me, she decided to revisit everything once more. I still to this day can't fully figure out why she even toyed with the idea of talking with me after what she had done. Who did she think she was, and why did she think it was okay to keep this charade going? Perhaps it was her way of finding peace with the whole ordeal by confirming if I had found mine. The letters she sent pried ever so gently into my life, weaving a new web of emotional instability within me and again causing sleepless nights and unsettling discomfort. I wanted her gone, forever, no longer deserving the right to do this to me. She was again continuing to take and not give back, causing pain, yet never trying to heal the wounds. All I wanted her to do was tell me it was over and to stop me from holding on to a hope that would never be fulfilled. She always managed to leave a door open, however, and this time I was shutting it. I would not let her avoid the issues any longer. She said her piece, and then I said mine. I slammed the door closed and figuratively walked away, hoping it was forever this time.

I think this is why I personally found such peace with my brother's plan. It wasn't a new plan or idea by any means, a very old one in fact, that many people for hundreds of years have already come up with. But this agenda offered the others, and myself, a foundation by which we could always turn to that we had otherwise overlooked. No matter what happened in the future, or where we ended up, we had a plan, we had a group of people we could rely on, and we would have the means to protect ourselves. A big part of me now can relate to the reasons why kids growing up fall into the gang style of life. That way of existence allows them to have a group of people they can rely on and a means to make sense of their lives when their families had fallen short.

However, we weren't some gang out to stake our claim or rough up the kids down the block. We had a focus, an itinerary of sorts, and each of us had a specific task to complete. Everyone involved would spend the next two years specializing in a unique skill. This particular talent was something determined by the collective group to be useful to everyone, and, if possible, something the individual was already skilled in. After the two years were finished each specialist would then make everyone else proficient with the same task. This way we always had a specialist, but if something happened to them we wouldn't be up a creek without a paddle.

Even though we decided most non-emergent things as a group by a majority vote, my oldest brother took the lead with everything else. It is proven that people need leadership when they group together; otherwise there would be too many ideas, directions, and solutions to every situation. People would argue, and the overall goal would be lost, replaced by cynicism and anger. So, to thwart all this we established a chain of command, and everyone abided by it, otherwise they could walk away. We did not sign contracts or negotiate deals with each other. My brother did not invite people into the group that required such things; instead, the group relied on the honor system. Nobody was outside of the rules established, and all were subjected to equal punishment based on any offense committed. Looking back on that period now I laugh; we never even came close to needing any of it. The honor system wasn't initiated in any of those men's lives on that particular day for the first time. All of the members lived a life of pride before, and none of them brought deceit to the table.

It's funny really, as we get older we reflect on our past and look at all the amazing things we have learned, and all the other things we managed to completely overlook. I remember being so ignorant of a lot of things, hell, I probably am still ignorant of a few and don't even realize it yet. Whatever the case may be, it truly shocks me to think how back then China was buying up land all over the United states as well as the rest of the world and no one seemed to care or notice. They all, including myself, shrugged it off as just a country trying to better itself and its people by helping the world prosper as well. Ignorance at its finest! My brother and a select few others didn't see it that way. When China purchased both ends of the Panama Canal and openly owned a major portion of the United State's debt, well, everything started falling into place. This pattern is what became known as the modern economic collapse forged by foreign and domestic interest. If you don't know this already, then shame on you for even being alive now after it has all ended. Good people died because of this gigantic mistake, people I called friends, and if you are too stupid to realize what happened and why, then you better not miss the points I am making now.

Look it up if you don't believe me. The information is out there, you just need to know the right questions to ask, one of which is what happened to the core of China before the collapse? Well, look into the massive ghost cities that were popping up all over that nation and the resulting impact it had on its people. That information alone is enough to find you a good understanding of the foundational mistakes made by all parties involved. Once the economy overseas started to fall apart, who do you think came looking for their money? When one party could not pay the other, who do you think closed down the Canal? As a result of the Canal closing, what kind of impact do you think that had on the shipping system? Enough said? I think so. The resulting outcome was a chain reaction fueled by stupidity, ego, ignorance, and a lack of forethought that brought the world to its knees. All we could do as a group was pray for the best and plan for the worst. This whole calamity did not happen overnight; it took years to raise high enough to crumble hard enough. Yet, in that time my brother's group was able to solidify its cohesiveness and become all that he had hoped for and more. I remember standing there in that grassy field years ago; looking back over my shoulder as we pressed through a burnt town looking for anything of value, people, food, so on and so forth. Watching the rest of my team move with such precision, grace, and silence was truly a sight to be seen. I was extremely proud to be with them and to have the opportunity to tell this story, even when the fighting and dying started. This was my calling, and without them I never would have realized it. But, I am getting ahead of myself.

Chapter 2

. . . The End Of The Old Ways . . .

When we started to get things rolling in the directions we wanted them to go, I tended to have very little free time. The times I did find myself without anything to do I would often daydream about anything and everything. Some of my thoughts would drift towards wondering what my ex was up to and whom she might be doing it with. I would wonder if she thought the same things about me, or perhaps she thought nothing of me anymore. Other times, and most of them, I would dream about the endless possibilities of how the world as we knew it would end and where I would be when the shit hit the fan. I never imagined killer zombies or asteroids destroying all mankind, rather, I dreamed about economic downfall and social arrest, or even the unbelievable idea of invading forces. Sure, those thoughts are dark and even pessimistic to a few. But to me, these thoughts are what kept me going. I never truly wanted them to happen, but a small part of me wished and rooted for them to come true. I didn't think this way because I wished harm on anyone. I simply didn't feel at home in this world anymore and felt strongly that we needed to wake up from the apathetic lifestyles in which we were choosing to live.

This group I found myself in over the past few years had become my family, and all the training, preparation, and determination needed to be used wisely, not wasted. I gradually plucked away at the job my brother helped get for me working at the local newspaper. It wasn't much, but it paid what little bills I had and kept my writing skills up to par. It also gave me the opportunity to travel around, not too far away, but far enough that I began to meet new people and make new friends. The old life began to fade, and this new life I was creating for myself started to make sense and wrap its figurative arms around me in a giant comfortable hug. I even became lackadaisical in certain areas, allowing the gas tank in my truck to go below half a tank on occasion. As time dragged on, a part of me started to feel as though all this planning was for nothing. I continued to keep my get-home-bag in my truck, along with my handgun locked away under the back seat. Yet, I didn't frequent the local gun range as often and missed a few of the group meetings. My actions didn't go unnoticed, but before my brother could approach me things took a turn for the worse.

Things didn't start off with a bang; rather they trickled in slowly and chipped away at our very societal core. First, the market started to dwindle after inflation had jumped once again. Then the countries that owned portions of our debt came looking for what was theirs. When they didn't find it they began to pressure our economy with diminished trade, vetoed visitation rights of our citizens, and finally over-taxation of our trading. The smaller countries could not push back hard enough, but larger ones could and soon enough found ways to push back with intensity. China was the worst along with the Middle East. The other countries like Australia, Britain, and some of the European nations negotiated and worked with us, some even went as far as forfeiting portions of our responsibility to pay back that debt. China, however, put their foot down and halted all trade with us, which in turn hurt them more than they anticipated. They also shut down our access to the Panama Canal. These steps, as well as moving troops onto our soil, began conflicted times for all parties involved. China claimed the troops were military analysts brought over to help the United States Federal Government, but we all really knew what was going on.

I personally believe that China's over extension within its own economy is what set the ball rolling on their end. If the Internet is still available where you are now, look up "China's Modern Ghost Cities." That topic alone may shed a little light on the subject. Once again, do the research for yourself; I am not here to teach or analyze statistics and historical hypothesis; I am merely here to inform you a little on the subject at hand. Whatever the case may be, the causes of what happened aren't important. What is important is that they did happen, and we were caught in the very middle of it. Those lazy mistakes I was talking about before, well, they came back to bite me in the ass and a hard bite it was. They almost cost me everything.

When things really started happening I was out of the area doing some stupid follow-up story on a flea market in the central valley area about two hundred miles away from home. Apparently this particular flea market had merchants that were caught selling guns to locals under the table. As a result of this, the law enforcement in the area began searching houses in the town door-to-door. As they did, they began taking inventory, and, at times, even went as far as confiscating any firearms they came across, regardless if they were properly owned or not. This created enormous outrage within the community, and multiple police involved shootings had taken place as a result on the invasion of privacy. The peculiar part about it was that the local police department had requested federal assistance with the increase in violence, yet they were told none would be coming. For some reason, it seemed the feds had bigger fish to fry and would be sitting out this particular small town quarrel.

I was there attempting to interview all parties involved when the bombings in San Francisco, Los Osos, Vandenberg Air Force Base, and several other dozen locations up and down the California coastline took place. Each target appeared to have specific reasons for being chosen, and more than likely the official reasons would never come to light. None of it mattered to me though. I knew what was happening, and as the news poured in from around the country it would only be a matter of time before things went from really bad to worse. I remember walking to my truck, not running or panicking, and driving the short distance back to my hotel. After parking, I stepped out into the sunlight, and for the first time in months felt completely alive. The sun felt warm, the air smelled crisp, and my feet were light. I opened up the rear door and grabbed my get-home-bag or GHB. I lugged it out of the back seat and carried it into my hotel feeling wonderful.

Sitting on the edge of my bed I pulled out my cell phone and stared at it for a few seconds. I hadn't been without it for as long as I can remember, saying goodbye now felt like saying goodbye to a good friend. I sent out my first and only alert text to the recording stations we had set up at our two checkpoints and the bug out location or BOL. My text included the following:

James, 205 miles away CP 1,

drive, walk,

GHB, SA,

1-5 days CP 1,

CP 2, BOL

The message I sent stated who I was, how far I was away from our established first checkpoint, that I would be able to drive most of the way, yet may finish on foot. It also included that I had my get-home-bag with me as well as my primary side arm. I anticipated that my travel time to the first checkpoint would take one to five days and that the team was not to wait for me there but rather meet with me at the second checkpoint or our BOL. Our group had come to an agreement that we were to create two checkpoints, or primary and secondary rendezvous locations, before ending up at the BOL, our home away from home. These checkpoints were locations off the beaten path, yet close enough to not be a hassle to get to. Their purpose was to stockpile supplies and ammo, and provide a safe place to rest up if any team member found himself there alone. They were temporary, very temporary, and were mainly there to give any member moving on foot a fighting chance at getting to our BOL.

Without them, the likelihood of making it several hundred miles was very poor.

After I sent this message I realized a few things, the primary and most intensive one was that I was now alone. No one was coming to help me, and I could not stop to help anyone else. My only objective was to arrive at CP1 and CP2 without any delay and within a two-week window for resupplies and assistance. After the two weeks were up, I had very little chance of finding any of the group members outside of the BOL. Family and friends were being gathered and moved as I was sitting there on the bed, and my only task was taking care of myself. If, however, everything that was now happening around me was just a bazaar coincidence, then we would continue on with the plan and wait out whatever this was at the safe house. Whatever this event happened to be, I was not about to sit around and find out; I needed to move, and fast. I pulled the battery from my phone and placed it and the phone in a prepaid envelope I had in my bag that was addressed to me. I left it on the bed with a note for the maid to please put it in the hotel's outgoing mail and stood up to change my clothes.

Once I was finished, I peered over at myself in the mirror. I looked good and felt ready for anything. I filled up all my water containers from the bathroom sink, and once I finished strapping on my weapons I moved outside and headed for my truck. I imagined I would step out into a world of chaos, as if everything had gone to complete shit since I went into my hotel room only moments ago. But, as I pulled open the door and allowed my eyes a moment to adjust in the sunlight, I saw that nothing was happening, no sirens could be heard, and I only saw a few people were out and about. The people I did see were just walking with a purpose, carrying grocery bags or listening to their iPods, and none of them seemed stressed about a thing. I decided not to dwell on it and opened my truck door and placed my bags back inside. As I sat down, I realized I might have a problem with my new attire. The gun strapped to my right thigh was now digging into the center console, and my machete on my back didn't offer enough leeway in terms of back support. I cursed myself for not preplanning this. I stepped back out of my truck, removed the blade on my back, and readjusted my sidearm as well as the armor surrounding my torso.

Sitting back down in my truck, things felt better but would take some getting used to. I closed the door, turned on the engine, and cursed myself again. How in the hell would I be able to travel two hundred plus miles on a quarter tank of gas? The statement, "I am an idiot," screamed in my head! I needed to fill up and quickly, before other people started getting the same idea. Off in the distance I could see a gas station in the general direction I needed to head, and without hesitation that was the direction I went. Apparently, however, a few people were indeed beginning to have the same idea I was. As I pulled into the station I barely beat an RV filled with angry white people and a minivan with what seemed like ten people inside that both careened into the lot. All three of us converged on this gas station at the same time, barely missing each other, and took the three remaining pumps. I swear I heard all three vehicle's tires screech to a halt.

The owner of the gas station had either already wised up by shut off his credit card machines, or his machines were just off by coincidence. Out in front of his store he placed a sign that clearly stated CASH ONLY. This, in turn, had created a small, angry mob right outside the minimart door, and once the RV and minivan pulled in the mob doubled in size. I cursed myself again. This could have been avoided if I only kept my tank above half like I was supposed to do. I locked my truck and paced myself as I approached the minimart. I saw him before he fired the shot, and I pulled my gun, taking cover and aiming directly at him. His shot had been fired straight up into the air as his partner yelled over the megaphone for the crowd to disperse. Neither of the officers counted on seeing me there, and once their eyes locked on me I remembered the story I was here to write for the newspaper. These cops already had a bad taste in their mouths in regards to locals with guns. Now here I was wearing one in the open, out in public, and in full body armor; this whole situation did not bode well for me.

"Everybody freeze! You with the gun! Drop your weapon and lay face down on the ground! Now!!" the officer with the shotgun yelled at me. I did not need this. I did not need to be locked up in some jail while the world fell apart around me. I also did not need a ton of angry cops chasing me across the state if these bombings did not turn out to be a national event. Meanwhile, as I crouched behind a gas pump the mob was dispersing rapidly around me. Everyone was running in different directions, and I saw my chance and I took it. I grabbed one of the teenage girls that was with the minivan and pulled her in front of me as a shield. Now, I am not proud of this one bit, but I did what I needed to do. I stood up and pulled my side arm and pointed it right at the officer with the shotgun. "You and I both know neither of us has time for this. All I came for is to PAY for my gas peacefully and be on my way out of this town. If I am able to do this, nothing will go wrong and NO ONE will get hurt."

I pulled the girl in tighter and positioned myself with my back to the minimart where I was able to watch the clerk, the mob, and the officers without making myself vulnerable to some nut bag want-a-be hero. With this adjustment on my part the second officer pulled his sidearm, and we now had ourselves an old-fashioned stand off. No one blinked, no one spoke, and no one moved. We all stood there silent for what seemed like an eternity. I saw the officer with the shotgun open his mouth to speak, yet shut it just as quickly without saying a thing. Great, I thought, I just screwed myself out of a clean getaway, and now I was going to have to kill these two cops. In my head the ridiculous notion of killing these officers was playing out and was interrupted when the mother of all explosions went off.

The ground shook and a huge fireball could be seen rising up into the air behind the officers about a mile away in the direction of City Hall. These bombings were no longer isolated. The officer with the shotgun must have been ex-military with combat experience because he neither flinched nor moved as the massive cloud of flames rose into the air and radiated heat in our direction. I will give the two of them credit, however, for the mere fact that neither of them looked at it, yet the officer with the megaphone seemed straight out of high school and looked about ready to burst with indecision. He wised up though and holstered his gun, telling his partner to do the same. Granted, the explosion was a considerable distance away, but the intensity of the blast could not be mistaken. His partner, however, did not follow suit. Instead, the officer with the shotgun took one step back and spoke to me. "I agree, there is more than this going on right now," as he gestured with a nod of his head in the direction of City Hall and smirked. "But, we are not going anywhere until we know these people are safe and you won't hurt them. You have my word we will leave if I have yours that these people will not be harmed by you."

I looked at him, told him he had my word, and waited for him to back off. It was not until he lowered his weapon that I let the girl go and did the same myself. We stood there looking at each other for a few painful seconds, like a couple of men back in the old Wild West sizing each other up as they passed by on horseback in some random prairie somewhere. The officers then got in their car and sped off in the direction of the explosion, leaving the rest of us to sort things out. I turned to the crowd now forming around the gas pumps and held up my weapon in their direction. "People, you have my word I won't shoot any of you if I can get my truck filled and be on my way, but I won't hesitate to shoot any and all of you if that does not happen. Understand!?" With that I pulled out two silver one-ounce coins and tossed them to the minimart clerk who stood near by, his mouth gaping in amazement at what just happened. I told him I wanted pump number four open, and he just looked at me, confused, until I aimed my gun at him and repeated my request. He then came back to reality and appreciated the situation by promptly freeing up my pump so that I could fuel my truck.

Before I even began the process I realized it would seem rather difficult to try and fill my tank while at the same time I was keeping one eye on the crowd and the other on the rest of the world. So, I enlisted the help of a not-so-willing young man in the front row. This particular young lad grumbled at my request, or rather demand, to fill my tank for me, but he reluctantly did so after his mother pushed him forward trying to keep the peace. I stood back; gun still raised, pointed in the direction of the mob, and surveyed the scene before me. The world was now slipping into disarray. Sirens could be heard in every direction and distant gunfire was becoming less and less a sporadic issue and more a constant one. I needed to get moving!

It seems that the stupid gas pumps move their slowest when you have some place to be. While pumping the gas, I could tell the adolescent young man was plotting multiple ways to end me, and it was obvious he had settled on an idea or two. I calmly leaned over so that he could hear me while no one else could and said, "Don't even think about it, you won't live to regret your decision, I promise you that; your mother over there needs your help, don't deprive her of that. Do we understand?" He squeezed the nozzle harder and released, finishing up the task at hand and returned the nozzle to its home.

The little bastard sulked over to his mother, appearing as though I had stolen something from him. He failed to see that I had not taken anything from him; rather I gave him something instead. I just provided him with a purpose in his life, which was to take care of his mother like all sons should do and something of which they should never need to be reminded. I wonder if he lived up to that responsibility once I left or did he revert back to his juvenile, selfish ways and wind up getting them both killed. No matter, I did not then and still don't concern myself with things like that. Everyone is held accountable for their actions some day, be it in this life or the one after. So why worry about others when I have my own shit, more often too much shit, with which to be concerned.

I made sure my gas tank was closed up properly and actually full, then I proceeded to curtsy mockingly in the direction of the gas station mob. I heard someone call me a dick from somewhere in the middle of the group as I jumped in my truck; shortly thereafter I was on the road and gathering speed. I needed to get out of here and away from this city and remain away from any other city for as long as I possibly could. The rapid progression of activity in the town I was just at, violent or not, signified that enough was going on now to distract everyone else from me and to cause enough unease within myself.

I had enough food on hand through MRE's and various other camping foods to last three weeks without rationing. I had enough water for one person to last at the very least a week without being strict. I was in good shape and potentially had 650 miles of road to travel before I reached the BOL. As mentioned before, I only had about 200 miles now to the first checkpoint and the ability to resupply. I could do this, barring any unforeseen circumstances like my truck breaking down; this would not be difficult. However, it was the unforeseen circumstances that were now becoming all too common, and the longer it took me to travel the rest of the way to the BOL, the more and more circumstances I would find. Or, perhaps these circumstances would find me.

Chapter 3

. . . A Look Back . . .

Our Bug Out Location turned out to be property the group acquired through a purchase made together. Buying property isn't always easy on one's own, yet pulling a couple dozen incomes together made the endeavor a breeze. We ended up settling on a 100-acre parcel with a two bedroom, one bath cabin already built on the property that was completely off the grid. Being off the grid wasn't a requirement, yet it made the purchase easier since it did not appeal to the larger portion of buyers on the market. It was, however, what we wanted from the get go.

Once we acquired the property, we went to work on making it the ultimate in long-term capability. Several of the group members were licensed contractors and began taking shifts amongst each other with retrofitting and outfitting the structures already on site. Once the buildings themselves were brought up to speed, they set out using bobcats and other tractors on the surrounding topography. Our goal was to make the property appear as though it was used primarily by the cabin and its occupants. The real occupancy on the property, however, would be constructed underground by basically digging a giant twelve-foot deep hole in the ground around the cabin that spanned at the very least an acre itself. Once the hole was dug, we would use thousands of cinderblocks and reinforced concrete to create a complicated housing, storage, and training facility completely hidden from view.

The last portion of construction involved all of us, and those two weeks we spent on the property together were some of the best times I had ever had. It was truly amazing to see just how much we accomplished as a working machine and how much fun we had in the process. I have never moved so many cinder blocks in my life, nor had I seen a construction site move with such speed. We accomplished the task at hand a solid week sooner than planned. As a result of the rapidity, we freed up the majority of the team and put them to work on finishing the crop fields with the left over dirt and as well as finalizing the guard pits. We shied away from guard towers because they tend to draw unwanted attention and settled on guard pits, sculpted into the surrounding, rolling hills.

The pits would be connected to the actual complex through tunnels dug out by the bobcat like many of the tunnels constructed during the Vietnam conflict. These tunnels would essentially be completely hidden from view above ground. Each tunnel would have several large steel doors between the pit and the complex itself, preventing any outside invasion if a pit was overrun. Each door would have a bulletproof sliding window built into it, allowing for clearance to be made prior to opening a door. With so many brilliant people in this group, we tended to think of everything. While this attribute was at most times beneficial, it also had a tendency to slow headway and bog down progression. One of the items that became a hindrance in our forward motion was the obsession with possible spy satellites finding our location. I won't tell you how we did it, but needless to say there will be no one spotting us from the sky any time soon.

Separate entrances to our complex were constructed in five other locations aside from the four guard pits, bringing the total number of entryways to nine. There was a tenth, but I am not going to mention anything more about that one. The closest entrance to the complex was nearly a hundred yards away, while the rest ranged from five hundred to a thousand yards away. Each of the tunnels leading from an entrance was equipped with decontamination chambers and four small 8-foot by 10-foot rooms. These rooms could be, and most likely would be, used for prisoner interrogation or guest housing. The reason for this was simple, no non-group member was allowed inside the complex unless unanimously voted in by the team itself, and everyone who made entry did so after being screened, member or not.

Team members and their families had solidified their residences within the complex through hard work, financial contribution, and being sworn in by my oldest brother. Anyone else who would come along after the complex was placed into lockdown mode would be subject to stringent interviews and investigations by preselected members. We were not a charity and would in no way resemble one to any onlooker. Individuals who did not prepare like we had, did not deserve the right to enjoy the fruits of our labor without just cause. There were, however, exceptions to this rule. We planned on rebuilding whatever was lost in our society one day if it came to that, and if people came along that would prove valuable in the future we would want to keep them around. We also had plans in place to recruit reinforcements for such times that we may need them. We wanted to train, educate, and arm the right people to expand our reach when the time came. We stocked an enormous amount of ammunition, weaponry, tactical clothing and equipment needed for such a task in an offsite location. When the time was right we would dip into this reserve and outfit the appropriate people for the tasks that would lie ahead of them.

No one entered this group by way of laziness or an accident of some sort. Each initial team member and their families did their fair share of the work, and everyone gave the same percentage of their income and time to the cause. Regardless of how much a family made in income, twenty percent of that was contributed to the cause. Granted, there were some who gave a lot while others seemed to give a little, but when it came down to it, everyone gave an equal share of what they had. The most important and valuable part of this agreement was that it was just that, an agreement. There were no disapprovals or quarrels created by this collection process. The group simply came to an understanding, and everyone involved felt it was more than fair.

We even went as far as to make it unacceptable for anyone to give more than what was required of them. This turned out to be more difficult than you might think. Everyone at times got excited about particular things and wanted to go above and beyond the normal dues. This had to be stifled to deter future arguments when things got really tight and the excess was no longer present. In all, the total of two years had come to an end, from the day my brother approached me with his idea to the final finishing touches on our "home away from home." I do remember vividly the last day of construction, when we loaded up the bobcat and subsequent tools for transportation to the second location. We were all very proud, dirty, but proud, and enjoyed the first fruits of our labor by toasting cheap champagne, which in turn gave most of us really bad headaches.

Our hard work and determination paid off, and we had created a safe place from which our closest friends and family could benefit. The only hard part now was bringing the family in on it. We had completed this entirely on our own, and Dylan, my third brother in the line of five, would be in charge of the vacuum-sealed packages we would give out to the family and friends we felt were good candidates. The sealed contents would include maps to the site, a list of items they needed to bring with them, and a compass with directions on how to use it. The map contained directions from wherever they resided and would only take them to the furthest entrance of the BOL, the one established for receiving with the bulk of the smaller rooms. Each package came with a printed and signed letter giving them detailed instructions on when to open the package and to otherwise leave it sealed and locked away.

Every team member and their immediate family had the opportunity to pick ten people, no questions asked, and another five that required group approval. This actually turned out to be more difficult than otherwise perceived. Most of the team members couldn't even come up with five people, much less fifteen, that they wanted to share and felt could add to our success. As a result of this phenomenon, the group settled on five guests per member, leaving the available housing for future prospects.

Everything we stored and collected was done so with the utmost care and precision. We did not want to be in any way short on anything, and at the same time, we didn't want to have too much of one thing or another. With this in mind, we decided to plan for a five-year stay in the complex without outside help. This meant storing enough food and water for, at the very least, the thirty priority team members and their five choices, which would total 180 people. This did not take into account the possible loss of life prior to arriving at the BOL and anyone who would add to that number once the complex was occupied.

It was not a matter of if we could get the food and water and other supplies; it was a matter of the possibility of not getting enough. Knowing my brother Eddie, we would go overboard, and that is just what we did. He heard the number 180 and scowled at it. He looked up at me during one of our many meetings and just stared. "We aren't going to even consider 180 as the final number, rather let's set our target at 300 and then move forward from there," he said. "That way if for some reason the five year mark is too short, we can remain indoors longer without any complications, not to mention the possibility of expansion or loss."

I was actually surprised by this number, as were a couple of the other members. No one to my knowledge had even considered anything beyond two hundred. Three hundred was a monstrous number and would take an incredible amount of time and effort to achieve. Yet, he remained firm with his assessment and somehow convinced everyone there that this was the number to reach. Howard was in charge of the logistical nightmare that was our situation, and I never envied his responsibilities. Often, I felt mine weren't on the same playing field as the rest, simply keeping a historical record to later be organized into a readable book, just didn't seem like enough. But, no one agreed with me. Everyone felt my job was just as important, if not more so, than the rest. I really did not see it the way they did, but I never hesitated to respect their opinions and perform the task given to me without complaint.

When my oldest brother Eddie projected that three hundred should be our goal, Howard simply doubled his projections and moved forward from there. It felt crude to the rest of us, but he wasn't by any means dumb, so we felt if it worked in his mind then it worked in ours. Everyone else had a task to tend to in the following months, and it was decided that we would meet back at our property midway through the year to finalize things. At this point we had the buildings and surrounding construction finished; it was now a matter of interior decorating and maintenance before the site became fully operational.

The outside structures may have looked and seemed crude, but the inside had to be pristine. There was no telling how long we might have to live in there, and no one was willing to do so in a prison. Our goal had to be making the facility enjoyable to live in regardless of how much time we would be spending in it. We tried to avoid this necessity by all means possible, yet we kept returning to it. We needed electricity to create a comfortable setting. It was that simple, yet that complicated in the same instance. How the heck would we do this without creating noise or drawing attention to ourselves? A generator required fuel at the very least, not to mention with an underground facility we would have exhaust to be concerned with and the obvious noise factor. Solar panels proved to be the best solution to the noise and exhaust issues, however, they aren't exactly appealing to the eye nor do they blend in well with nature.

You would be surprised just how big a hundred acres can be, and at the same time just how small it is from the air. The last thing we wanted was to have a solar panel array too close to the facility that we would be found out, and at the same time we did not want it too far away that it could be tampered with unannounced to us. Roger, a tech specialist that Chaz met while serving overseas, said that he knew of a dull, blacked out, solar panel not yet available to the public that he could acquire. The neat thing about these panels is that they didn't reflect away nearly as much light as the ordinary blue colored ones do. In turn, you can place these panels almost anywhere and they will draw in just as much, if not more, than the original widely used panels.

With this new feature at our fingertips, we decided to divide the large array of panels into six smaller arrays and place them throughout the property. Each of these sections would be visible from one, two, or three of the lookouts and could be checked on daily. At the same time, splitting the sections up allowed for maximum protection in case they became a target. Because the panels did not require direct sunlight, they could be placed in areas of hiding. Some went into the tree lines, others on the ridge rock, and the last remaining six went on the cabin roof with a few smaller wind turbines for a little added boost. In the beginning we had wanted to make the cabin look like a run-of-the-mill urban survivalist's shitty attempt at a get-away. After a while it became fun to think of cheesy things to put in it, but at the same time it was our cover story and had to draw little attention, which meant it couldn't be so grandiose in style.

The majority of our members lived in the lower portion of the state, and thus figuring out the locations for the checkpoints was not a difficult task. Moreover, finding storage facilities off the beaten path turned out to be the tricky part. We couldn't just pick any old storage locker facility. We needed places away from passersby and not very accessible by the general public. Believe it or not, these places do exist, and they cater to clients such as ourselves, people looking to hide their belongings and not just store them.

We found two locations perfect for our endeavor and set up long-term accounts with both of them, and in doing so we were able to receive a considerable discount. Since we confirmed five consecutive years of storage with the option to renew at each facility, they cut the cost in half. We paid the first 2 years upfront and signed contracts for the following three years, which would be paid out in monthly installments. Our group secured two 10x20 lockers at each location that were adjacent to each other. We then proceeded to place a doorway in the wall dividing the two rooms, unannounced to the owners, thus creating one room for vehicle and fuel storage and the other room for supply storage and sleeping quarters.

The team fortified the living side of the storage rooms and secured the doors, making them inoperable from the outside. We built several sleeping bunks, enough to sleep eight people comfortably, within the living quarters and then set up an exorbitant amount of shelving space. Once the team members requiring the help from these checkpoints arrived at them, they would park their vehicle inside the first storage room and then proceed to rest in the second before continuing on their journey to the hideout. It seems simple enough, but the pure amount of time and effort that went into preparing these two locations almost dwarfed the energy spent on the bug out location.

There was a lot of bickering that took place when we picked the two storage locations. People started to get a little selfish and wanted them closer or perhaps farther away from their start off points. Eventually, Eddie brought out a state map and drew two circles around our BOL. One circle resided two hundred miles away from the BOL and the second circle sat at the four hundred mile mark. He then took a poll of the already plotted travel paths to the BOL for each team member and placed two tacks on the paper signifying the two locations we would place the checkpoints. That actually silenced everyone involved in the quarreling, which surprised me. I remember thinking then that the team had been working so well together, and for quite some time, that perhaps we had gotten to a point where we were trying to find things to fight about, even as arbitrary as to where to put something most would not even use.

Yes, none of us actually believed we would need to use the checkpoint, yet all of us understood their importance and necessity. Everyone had their own idea and format for their plans on how to get themselves and their families to the BOL when the time called for it. Some of them would create the contents of a checkpoint on a covered trailer at their house and bring it with them. Others created modified vehicles with the ability to store larger than normal amounts of fuel. Whatever the case was, it had been decided that the responsibility of getting a team member and their families to the BOL was solely the responsibility of that team member and their family. Beyond that, it was every man for himself before you got the to the BOL. Yet, once you arrived, the team aspect kicked in, and no one was left behind. Obviously, if you ran across a team member stranded along the way you would help them out, but besides that scenario there weren't many other options for help.

The main point is, though, that the group decided as a whole that no full group effort would be made regarding the preparation of each individual team member's escape and evasion process. Each team member's ability to get to the

BOL was their responsibility and theirs alone. That is where I found myself now, on the road headed to the first checkpoint and alone, wishing I had prepared more, hoping I had prepared enough. I had a long way to go still, and my mind raced with the possibilities that awaited me.

Chapter 4

. . . The Lonely Road . . .

One of the things I so vividly recall from childhood was the story telling days. The moments you would be with friends and each of you would have some kind of adventure to share about. The best were always when school was back in from the summer, and each kid tried to one-up the next with what they had done for fun during their vacation. After a while the stories just got out of hand and the exaggeration would soar to new heights. However, one phrase that was always yelled out in chorus in response to an outlandish story was the line, "No way! I'd have to see that to believe it." And it was true, there just were some stories that were told by my friends that were either totally made up or you truly couldn't believe what they were saying happened unless you were there to see it yourself.

As I drove now, and the sights all around me came flooding in, I could not even believe what I was seeing, and that is just it, I was seeing it. Most of what was happening was reactive action by regular people. The media had come a long way over the years and now its fear-based programming had warped reality in a way that almost made it unbearable to deal with.

Over amplification of normal events such as car accidents, crime rates, unemployment, and turmoil overseas had changed the way people dealt with things on a normal day-to-day basis. People had forgotten how to talk to their neighbors, to trust each other with simple things, and to think for themselves. As a whole, society wasn't the brightest crayon in the box, it was more so a defective, inoperable pair of scissors that were otherwise useless yet everyone struggled to use them.

It is true though, no matter how you cut it, people as a whole are dumb and react poorly to stress. It has been said before that a person, one lone individual, is smart, and this is very true. One person, given time and opportunity, can accomplish almost anything with enough willpower and enthusiasm. However, you throw a group of people into any situation and induce a little panic, and all hell breaks lose. Utter insanity spews forth and the reactions become costly, yet valueless, and nothing that comes from them is useful. People suffer at the hands of indecision or violence brought on by misinterpretation of their surroundings and the actions of others. So true I thought, as I gazed at the billowing smoke towers in the distance, the cars speeding all around in every direction. Accidents had clogged one-way streets, and emergency crews faded in amongst the chaos. As I passed over a town from the raised freeway I could just make out a mob storming a grocery store and a half dozen police cars in the middle of the mix. The only detail I could see through the waving arms, flying objects, and occasional body jumping off a parked car into the writhing crowd, were police hats and flaying nightsticks. The first responder world was in a shambles, and the sooner the cops, medics, and firefighters realized it, the safer they would be. They needed to mobilize in one location and then assess the situation. Responding the way they always did at this time was fruitless. I could only imagine some of the horrors already playing out in every small town up and down the state.

My front passenger tire hit dirt as it left the asphalt and signaled me to pay attention to where I was headed. I chuckled a little at the thought of crashing my truck at a time like this as I slowed and eased back onto the pavement. What a bonehead move that would be to lose focus right now. I peered in my mirror and watched as the dust cloud I made gave way to a fast moving four-door sedan coming up behind me. The lights were not lit on this vehicle, and they were easily going twenty miles faster than I was in my same lane. As they approached I slowly unlocked my gun and removed it from my holster, letting it rest in my hand on my lap. I leaned back into my seat and allowed the driver side pillar to hide my head. The sun was still out yet the dusky nature in the sky was making it more and more difficult to see without the help of headlights. I had planned on waiting to turn mine on at the last possible second to avoid attracting unwanted attention, yet now seemed like as good a time as any to turn them on. The car behind me switched lanes as my headlights came on, and as they began to move up along my left side I tapped the breaks and let them fly by.

They seemed to pay no attention to me and kept on going. The sedan looked like a late model Toyota with all the rear windows tinted black and from the looks of it, as they passed my headlights, had two or three people sitting inside. Several dozen yards ahead of me they switched lanes again back into mine and even went as far as using their right turn signal. I could see they could not close their trunk all the way and resorted to tying it down with bungee cords and rope. I holstered my gun and leaned forward back to where I usually sit when I drive and let myself relax a little. The dark car ahead of me turned their lights on and seemed to speed up even more, putting distance between us. Good, I thought, last thing I need is to be part of an improvised caravan.

People were panicking all over, that much was obvious, but I don't think at this point it permeated into every social aspect we have. The freeways seemed clear; traffic was light for this time of day, and for the most part seemed unaffected by what was going on. Perhaps people had not decided to run for the hills yet or maybe they didn't have hills to run to. Whatever the case, I was thankful and checked the clock, 7:35pm; I had about two hours to go before I could rest at the first checkpoint. Things looked good so far, let's just hope they stay that way.

The car was far enough away from me now to not be seen constantly as the road began to start winding through the hills. Every so often I would see their lights off in the distance through the low lying trees and then they would disappear again around another corner. There was some traffic headed in the opposite direction from me, not much, but enough to notice. I had been on the road maybe an hour now and had seen perhaps only a dozen or so cars heading in the direction I came from. The road began to twist and turn sharply as the jagged hillside stuck out the higher up in elevation I went. I remember driving this road a couple years back and thinking it would be fun to take a motorcycle on it and try to drag a knee around these corners. The roads were well taken care of and had little in the way of loose gravel or potholes. Maybe I would come back here some day if things turned out for the better; I'd like to think I would have that chance.

I saw her lying on the road ahead of me on the oil slick of my lane as I came around the bend. My headlights lit up her face and I could see her cheeks soaked in tears as her mascara ran down her face. I slammed on my breaks, stopping twenty feet from her and one hundred feet or so from the men. The sedan that passed me had pulled over to the side of the road about a hundred yards or so past her, and three men were half walking, half running towards her. I looked past them and saw their trunk was open, the cords that had held it closed appeared torn and frayed. The three men stopped walking, frozen in mid stride, seemingly waiting for my next move.

I knew what this was, and they failed miserably at it. It must have been their first time taking advantage of a woman, or at least they were rushed this time. Whatever they planned to do with this girl, she wanted no part of it. Appearing to have cut her way some how out of their trunk, she had then thrown herself out of a moving vehicle onto the concrete. Apparently, that was the better choice in her mind. I also did not ignore the fact that this could be a set up. They could have planned this to lure me into some kind of roadside robbery. That definitely was not going to happen, so I needed to maintain control of this shit storm. After stopping my truck, I made sure I kept the headlights on everyone while flipping my high beams on. I stepped out, drawing my weapon and using my door as a shield. None of them moved.

I talked to the girl first over the sound of my engine, asking her if she could walk. She said she thought so and attempted to stand. Once she was to her feet I asked her to lift her shirt and spin around, showing me she had no weapons on her. She wore dark blue mid-thigh shorts, a white t-shirt and tennis shoes without socks. Once I was convinced she had nothing on her that could hurt me, I instructed her to get in the passenger side and put on her seatbelt. I then devoted all my attention to the three men still frozen in the road.

They had begun to spread out on the roadway. They all appeared to be in their mid to late thirties, wearing jeans, t-shirts, and work boots of various colors and sizes. I yelled at them to lie down on the ground and not move. After that order bellowed from my lungs the two men closest to the oncoming lane crossed the road and jumped off the side. From the looks of it, they would land easily on the hillside below and make their way down the hill without incident. The third man, however, pulled a rather large knife from his waistline and yelled something to me in Spanish that I knew was nothing to be repeated to someone's mother. Holstering my gun I got back in my truck and floored it in his direction. He ran out of the way, just like I knew he would. Their vehicle was parked half way on the road and the other half partially in a turnout allowing me to pull up next to it on my side.

I proceeded to shoot out both of the passenger side tires as well as putt a few rounds into the engine block before pulling back onto the road and continuing forward. As I looked in my rear view mirror I could still see the third man standing in the road, knife in hand, watching me drive away.

I planned on putting some good distance between those men and myself before I thought about stopping again. That whole situation had not taken much longer than a couple minutes, yet it felt like an eternity. My hands were shaking and my head was racing. The adrenaline was catching up with me and I needed to slow it down. This was not what I wanted to run into nor had I planned on picking anyone up along the way. I looked over at her and saw that she was cowering against the door, seeming to attend to her wounds and ignoring me completely. She looked to be in her early twenties, white with dark brown hair and freckles. She was pretty, or at least looked like she could be when she wasn't looking beat up and covered in gravel. I told her there was water and something to eat in the passenger-side door compartment. She reached for the water and drank it all in seconds. I pointed out the second bottle and she repeated the action. She wiped off her mouth and sat back crying.

I turned back to the road ahead and gave her time to deal with whatever she was dealing with; I had some thinking to do anyways. Was I going to let her tag along or did I need to get rid of her as soon as possible? Various other questions raced through my head, some that I wasn't too proud of but what could I do, I am a guy and there are just some thoughts that are unavoidable. The first checkpoint would have clothing, food, the ability to get cleaned up, and so on. If anything, it would be best for me to take her there just so she would have a fighting chance if I decided to not take her with me, at least it would be the decent thing to do. While I went about justifying future actions in my head, I could hear her devouring the protein bar as she sat in the seat next to mine. It sounded like she hadn't eaten in a while. She didn't look malnourished, so this must have been a recent thing she went through I concluded. I'll ask her about it later if it feels right, otherwise, I could not care less about what happened to her; I am just thankful she is safe now, whoever she is.

I sat feeling proud as we drove. I had legitimately saved someone from certain suffering, all by myself. I deserved some kind of recognition for this I thought. Why hasn't she thanked me yet? Then again, I seriously can be a selfish prick sometimes and quickly stifled any egotistical inner thoughts. "My name is Phoebe," she said quietly. "Thank you for what you did back there . . ." I sensed she fell asleep after those words because her breathing became soft and drawn out. Her legs were curled up already, and she leaned against the door with her arms under her head. I locked the doors and pulled a blanket from the back and covered her with it. The road began to straighten out as the hills faded behind us. How metaphorically quaint this is, perhaps the straightening road would bring a little more peaceful monotony our way. I was quickly running out of room in my truck. I did not have the luxury of handing out seats all day long on this ride.

Time passed and as we pressed on I found myself drifting in and out of focus. My head was full and every time a new thought entered, my concentration dimmed a little more. I started to wander down the road of "what ifs" concerning myself with issues I could not change. I started to wonder how my brothers were doing, how my parents and the remaining other family members were faring, and I even thought about my ex. I was really tired of doing that, but she just seemed to always make her way back into my thoughts, no matter how hard I tried to push her out. I secretly hoped she was okay, while at the same time wished she might find trouble. Only then would I fantasize about coming along and whisking her off to safety and becoming the hero every boy dreamed they would be some day. Maybe then, I thought, she would take me back.

I cannot even begin to calculate how many dreams I dreamt up during my younger years. Most often those dreams were about being the hero, about saving the girl, and rescuing the helpless. Its amazing just how vital those aspirations are to a young man; they give him hope that there could be, and very well is, a better world out there for him. Those dreams sure as hell allowed me to think that I could change things some day, and at that, change them for the better. When I dreamt, the world did not seem as dark and dreary as it sometimes can be, certainly not as dark as it turned out to be in reality. Yet, reality really does have a way of stifling a young man's imagination, so much so that his hopes and aspirations become an unbearable weight that he cannot always carry beyond his youth. All too often, that boy settles into manhood broken down, bitter, and angry at a world that required him to settle and make compromises. He then sits and watches as that world steals all he had to give and vomits it back at him.

I hated that I thought of her still, more so that I thought of her at all. The energy alone that I spent mulling over what she did to me continually frustrates me to no end. What unimaginable other things I could have accomplished with that energy. Instead, I spent the last three years at half speed, moving forward with my life slower than I could be. There were days I just simply got up out of bed because I couldn't think of anything better to do. Most other days I didn't even try getting out of bed. I am amazed at what she did to me, it was as if she placed some sort of bomb inside my soul, inside the inner workings of who I was as a person, and when she kicked me to the curb with one last final flip of her finger, she set off that bomb and it utterly destroyed me. What else could I do, I thought, to make this pain go away? I had tried a lot of things, alcohol, anonymous sex with a few girls I'd rather forget, countless hours of exercise, this preparation with my brothers, and countless other things without effect. Sure, they helped for the time being by distracting me, but I always found myself alone, beaten and torn up, sitting by myself on the edge of my bed the next morning, wondering what in the hell I was going to do and wishing I had done none of it.

There were even times I looked over at the dresser drawer where I kept my gun and thought about blowing my brains out, at least that would silence the pain. Then again, my curiosity for the coming day squelched those negative thoughts enough so that I was able to continue on. It was like she cut off my leg when she left, literally giving me one less leg to stand on. At times I would forget what she did and fall right over, cursing her name as I hit the metaphorical ground. God, I hated it all so much! I wanted to scream all the air out of my lungs sitting here in this truck, maybe then I might feel a little better. Phoebe coughed quietly and brought me back down to reality. She opened her eyes and slowly sat up, having been asleep now for little over an hour. She adjusted herself in her seat and rested her head on her hand, leaning on her arm that was against her door. She looked over at me, and I noticed her eyes were strikingly green, bright even, amongst the tearstains she still had on her cheeks.

She attempted a smile, yet failed due to her lack of commitment. I did wonder about this girl and what her story was. A part of me really didn't give a shit though and wished she wasn't here. However, amidst my anguish I could be nothing other than the good guy, no matter how much suffering I would go through because of it, or that I would most likely finish last, if at all. I could be nothing else other than trustworthy, despite my darkest, innermost desires to be the bad guy everyone loved to hate. "My name is James by the way, thought you might want to know that," I said, looking away from her back to the road ahead.

"Nice to meet you, James, mind if I ask where we are headed?" I looked over at her; she was not looking at me but rather out the window, most likely searching for something she might recognize in the way of landmarks.

"That depends, Phoebe, on where it is you want to go, and more so on whether or not I want to take you there." I surprised myself at how cold the words were that came out of me, yet I continued. "I have a set agenda that's taking me several hundred miles north. I plan to stop driving in about an hour or so for the night; you're welcome to accompany me there and then make your decision after I get resupplied. But as far as I am concerned where you are going is up to you."

She peered over at me and didn't miss a beat. "Where are you planning to stop, and what's with the resupply mumbo jumbo, are you some sort of military soldier wannabe?"

Apparently the look I gave her silenced any more sarcastic remarks she planned to make. "How about this, Phoebe, I won't ask you about why you were in the trunk of that car or what you have been up to the past day or so, and you don't ask me any more stupid, condescending questions like that? Fair enough?" With that she looked back out the window and bottled up, not wanting to continue this line of conversation with me. What a bitch, I thought, she already forgot where the hell she had come from.

The remainder of the trip was uneventful; she mostly kept to herself, besides asking about another bottle of water, and I had a mountain of thoughts to tackle. When we arrived at the storage facility she was taken aback, and I could tell she became a little tense. The location we chose did not have an automatic entry gate and required a visitor to get out of their car, manually open the gate, drive through, and then close the gate before moving on to their unit. When I pulled up I turned off the truck, told Phoebe to remain in her seat, and stepped out into the cool night air, bringing the keys with me. We were far enough away from the closest downtown area and noise wasn't an issue out here. In fact, I couldn't hear a damn thing, which was a little unnerving to say the least. A lifetime of city noise suddenly gone made adapting to the silence a little more difficult than I anticipated it would be. I looked over at her, sitting their awkwardly in the front seat and could see she was nervous, not knowing what to expect, and definitely not expecting me to have come to a place like this.

"Relax. We are staying here for the night, you'll see. Just be patient and keep an open mind," I said as I started walking over to the gate. The lock was still intact and required a combination I had memorized ages ago. I input it and opened the gate, fighting a couple weeks of rust on the wheels, yet managing to make it appear effortless. The gun in my thigh holster felt good to wear. I had gotten so used to it over the years that when I didn't wear it I felt naked and vulnerable. During the past several hours I had felt more alive then I ever had; this was good for me, finally I was fitting into my own skin.

Once the gate was opened, I moved the truck through and then reversed the process. We then pulled into the four-acre lot of storage units and zigzagged through till we reached our two. The difficulty in opening the gate signaled to me that most likely I was the first and only user of this checkpoint so far. However, I would not take any chances and needed to approach as if under surveillance and maintain awareness of everything. The last thing I needed was to get gunned down by one of our teammates who happened to be a little trigger happy protecting his and his own.

I stopped shy of the next corner having turned off my headlights a hundred yards back or so. I told Phoebe to stay put, looked her straight in the eyes and made sure she understood. "You have no reason to trust me other than my actions thus far, that much I understand, but I need you to try hard right now and give me a chance to make sure we will be safe for the night." With that I handed her the keys, told her if something was to happen to me to take the truck and ram the front gate and drive until she ran out of gas. She looked more than frightened; yet an air of confidence told me she could handle it. I again exited into the night air, took a slow, deep breath, drew my weapon and slowly closed the truck door. I pied the first and only corner I came to by peering around it from a distance of six feet and stepping sideways as I did so giving myself the chance to clear any blind spots that corner created. Soon thereafter I crossed the narrow road, and began approaching our unit from the east, having parked the truck to the southeast. When I approached the first door I knelt down and tapped my knuckles against the lower corner of the living quarters side. I heard no sounds come from inside, nor did I get any feeling anyone was inside. I proceeded past the first roll up door and repeated the process on the vehicle parking side. Again, I heard nothing and got no real vibe that anyone was inside.

Lastly, I unlocked the parking unit, entered and did a quick search of both units, again pieing any corners I came to. No one was inside and everything was as it should be. Nothing inside the units appeared to have been used or tampered with, and I didn't get the feeling it was unsafe to be there. One thing my brothers always encouraged me to do was trust my gut feeling. It was all we had sometimes that gave us the upper hand in a given situation. Not the most scientifically reliable process of elimination, but trusting your own gut feeling can be a lifesaver and the one thing that can make or break you. I made my way back to the truck with as much caution as I had when I left. I found Phoebe still sitting in the passenger seat, seemingly very determined to believe that I would return. As I approached she opened her door and tossed me the keys, "I can't drive a stick anyways," she said, sitting back into her seat and closing the door. I got in and moved the truck around to the unit and backed into the space, leaving me enough room to fill up my tank. That was the first thing I did when I got out of the truck, using the canisters that were stacked up in the back of the unit. She got out and came around to my side and watched me while I emptied three five-gallon canisters into my tank.

Once I was finished, I marked and dated the canisters as empty and then closed the roll-up door, having left it open this long to ventilate. Once the door was closed I pulled out a flashlight and ran right into Phoebe who apparently had been following me around the room while I worked. The light lit up her face and I stepped back startled. "Holy crap, Phoebe, why are you right on my ass?" I smirked at her, which she couldn't see in the dark and told her to follow me into the next room. When I opened the door and flipped on the lights, and heard her gasp. The room was obviously not what she expected. With food and water filling up the front, ammo, armor, and a few weapons spaced out in the middle, and sleeping arrangements in back, this room was all we would need, and yet didn't feel the slightest like home. I made my way into the room and got started on picking out my armor and rifle for the coming day. As I worked,

I noticed she hadn't moved from the doorway. I stopped what I was doing and looked at her, "Yes," I asked impatiently. "What seems to be the matter?"

She just stood there, looking dumbfounded and speechless. "What is this place and who are you?" the words barely escaped her lips as she fidgeted with her hands. I set the rifle down and turned to face her, leaning back on the shelving units now at my back and crossed my arms, never taking my eyes of her.

"You ever see that cartoon growing up about the grasshopper and the ants? You know, the one where the ants are storing food and supplies all spring, summer, and fall in preparation for the long cold winter. Meanwhile, the grasshopper makes fun of the ants and tells them they need to have more fun and are just wasting their time. You remember that cartoon, Phoebe?" She nodded yes, still not having moved from the doorway. "We are the ants, Phoebe, my brothers and friends. We worked, while everyone else played." With that I resumed tasks at hand getting all my supplies ready for the next day before I sat down to eat and rest.

"But . . ." she stopped for a second and I peered over at her out of the corner of my eye while I continued to work. "But why are we here? Why aren't we in a hotel or why haven't we gone to the police? I do not understand why I can't just call my parents and have them come get me? Has something happened, James?"

I pushed a thirty round magazine into the AR-15 I chose to take with me and racked a round into the chamber. I carried the gun across the room, and she stepped out of my way as I secured it in the cab area behind my seat in the truck. As I did this I asked her how long she had been held captive by those men I found her with. She said they grabbed her when she left her car in the parking lot of her college that morning. She had been in the trunk ever since, and they were on the road a long time stopping only a couple times for gas.

I stopped her short, "So, you're telling me you have no idea what is going on in the world right now?" She shook her head slowly. "Phoebe, I personally saw three towns with active riots, large scale explosions, and raging, out of control fires since around ten this morning. I know of at least a dozen more explosions all over the state that were broadcasted on the news I saw before I left my hotel earlier today. These were coordinated attacks, not accidents, and from the looks, sounds, smells, and feelings of it all, the world as we know it is changing and changing drastically right now." I gave her a second to register all that I had said before continuing. "That is why, Phoebe, that we are not going to the police about what happened to you just yet, that is also why we are here at this place rather than a hotel. If you want to call your folks be my guest, there isn't a phone here and I tossed mine out the second I committed to this trip this morning. I assume if you had a phone you would have called a long time ago." I could tell I struck a nerve there; either she had called and no one answered or the men took her phone and with it her invisible lifeline that so many others in our generation had learned to not live without.

"I guess this is as good a time as any to figure out what you are going to do," I said, continuing to pack. "I, on the other hand, need to finish getting ready for tomorrow. Eat if you are hungry, drink if you need to, there is a bathroom in back if you need to go and if you are tired grab one of the bunks over there," I said pointing to the bunk bed system we constructed in the back.

I resumed my work and at the same time observed her in my peripheral vision. It must have been frightening to be told the world as she knew it was in turmoil, and she had no way to prove otherwise. Not having a phone to quickly look up the latest news or call a loved one can be a little disconcerting, to say the least. She walked over to one of the bunks and sat down. She then proceeded to lie down on her back and roll over to face the wall, curling up and bringing her knees to her chest. That was the last movement or sound she made while I was still up moving about. I didn't hear her the rest of the night, even though I made noise busying myself with the things I needed to get done before tomorrow. When I myself got into one of the bunks to rest for a few hours, I could just barely hear her faintly breathing, yet breathing nonetheless. Tomorrow is a new day, I thought, there is no rest for the weary, but there is for the prepared. I fell asleep easily that night, not because I was tired or run down, but because I had a clear head. Even though the world outside was in pandemonium, the biggest part of me didn't care about them, only who was in this room right now, and who was or would be at the BOL when I got there.

Chapter 5

. . . On the first day there was light . . .

Phoebe was still asleep when I awoke the next morning. The sun was barely up, and I wanted to see it rise on the first day of my adventure. I nudged with my hand on her shoulder and she jerked awake, looking at me with the puzzlement of a newborn, not knowing where she was. "I am going up on the roof, okay. I want to watch the sun rise and see what I can see." With that I headed outside and could hear her attempting to do the same behind me. When I rolled up the door where my truck was parked, I had my handgun ready in my right hand as I raised the door with my left and crouched. The cool air hit me with a chill, yet it smelled fresh. Not a soul in sight as far as I could see. The sky looked like it was on fire with orange and red colors so bright that they seemed to dance in every direction. I racked my brain as to when I had seen the sky like this before. The ladder to the roof was at the eastern most side of the building, back in the direction of where I parked the truck last night when I checked out the units. I made my way there, gun still in hand and making sure no one snuck up on me.

As I rounded the corner at the end of the building I could see Phoebe exiting the unit and looking for me. Before I left her field of vision I whistled to her and waved her over. I stopped waiting when I saw how slow she was walking. Dammit, if she was going to stick around she would need to change a few things and get her head out of her ass. I reached the ladder in no time and climbed with ease all the way to the top. The roof was a flat tar roof with gravel and crunched under the weight of my footsteps. Once I had found a place to look from I was taken aback at what I saw. In every direction there was an incredible amount of smoke in the air. Having hit the inversion layer as it rose, the smoke began to spread out in all directions, flying fast with the wind currents. Because of the smoke, the color from the sun in the sky was amazing. Purples, reds, oranges, yellows, and even blues blended together and created an amazing spectacle. I suddenly remembered why the colors seemed familiar to me; it looked like a large-scale wild-land fire had been brewing for weeks. Yet, this amount of smoke had been made in only a few hours.

I could hear Phoebe mutter a "wow" in response to what she saw. "Pretty crazy huh," I said in reply. "Everything looks like it is miles away from us, so I imagine we will be ok for a little while if we get on the road soon. You hungry?" She looked at me funny and said yes. "Good, this may be the last chance we have at eating a hot meal for a little while, might as well enjoy it while we can." I headed to the ladder and she grabbed my forearm as I passed her. I stopped and looked at her only to be given a hug.

"Thank you," she said. "I did not really tell you how thankful I am and was last night and I needed to this morning." I reciprocated and released quickly so that I could maintain some space between us. I was not in the mood right now for this; I needed to keep my head in the game.

"You're welcome, lets eat ok, we don't have much time." As I swung around onto the ladder I could see she was still taking in the sights. "You coming?" I asked, continuing my descent.

"James, I want to stay with you if that's okay." I stopped moving down the ladder and pushed myself back up just enough so that she could see I was listening. "I would like to stay with you and continue on; if everything you told me last night is true, I won't last a few hours on my own. Can I stay with you? Please?"

I looked at her and probably cocked my head to one side as I told her to come down off the roof and eat with me. "We can talk things over inside, okay." I grabbed the sides of the ladder and slid down landing quickly on the ground and removed my sidearm from its thigh holster for the walk back to the unit. I could hear her making her way off the roof behind me but was lost in my own thoughts for the time being. Great, a single guy with a ball and chain, this should make for an interesting trip to the BOL. I already broke rule number one, which was not to stop and help anyone. I wonder what other bright ideas I had in store for myself.

Once she came back inside, I had her close the roll up door behind her. We sat in silence, eating the breakfast I threw together using the hotplate connected to the array of car batteries on one of the shelves. Canned fruit, dehydrated powdered eggs, and some spam can go a long way in boosting morale. I looked across the table at Phoebe as she sat, staring down at her food and eating quietly. She was not the biggest or toughest looking girl I'd ever seen, but there was something about her that told me she could take care of herself. I couldn't quite put my finger on it just yet, but I got the feeling she wasn't completely useless, given the time and opportunity to prove it. Something in her eyes seemed to emanate wisdom beyond her years.

"You know, we are going to have to get you some clean clothes for the trip, what you have on won't cut it for much longer, especially if we will need to walk any part of it." She looked up at me and almost tossed the small table in my lap as she tried to give me a hug reaching over it. "Alright, alright just finish up your food. I will take a look and see what we have here in the way of female friendly clothing." I didn't get much farther than half way across the room when it dawned on me. "You ever shot a gun, Phoebe?" I asked turning around to face her.

"Uh, no, never thought I needed to know how. Why, is that going to be an issue?" She grabbed her plate and gathered up the other trash to put in a bag for the dumpster on our departure.

"No, not just yet, but we will need to make sure you know how eventually. For now I have a revolver here you can carry. Pretty basic, just point and shoot. Let's pray you will not have to though, till we can get some practice in at least." The only things I could find that would fit her from our clothing stash were some tan cargo pants and a black polo t-shirt, which happened to be the same thing I was wearing at the moment. Great, that is exactly what we need, to look official.

I turned around to hand them to her and she smiled. "How cute, we can match." She went to the back after taking them from me and changed. She got cleaned up the best she could while I finished up loading the truck and making sure everything was better than we had found it in the storage unit. It was now just after six in the morning, we had about four hundred more miles to go and one checkpoint left before we reached the end of our journey.

What I wanted to do was drive the whole rest of the way to the BOL today, stopping only for gas at the checkpoint. If it was at all possible we could forego the checkpoint and hit up a gas station instead. The possibilities were endless when it came to what we would find closer to a populated area, so I didn't want that to be my first plan. I did not want to use up our supplies, though, if I didn't need to. Yet, it would be so much easier to use the next storage unit instead of taking a chance on purchasing some gas. I had been lost in the internal dialogue within myself when it finally dawned on me. Where was Phoebe? I looked around the storage unit. I was still finishing up the final packing and preparation for our trip and she wasn't anywhere to be found. What the hell? I looked over at my truck and could see daylight. No freaking way! She went outside? Now? I set down the backpack I was loading and walked over to the doorway, and I was pissed. "Phoebe, what are you doing? We need to get ready, this isn't helping." I rounded the corner and something connected with my head, hard. Darkness enveloped me as I fell to the ground, striking my head on the concrete, even harder. And then, the lights went out . . .

I was surrounded by an almost tangible blackness in the sea of my own subconscious. I could taste the blood that flowed from a wound somewhere on my head right into my mouth, yet I could not see anything. Oh wow, it hurt a lot to open my eyes, I am not going to do that again any time soon. What happened?

What was going on? Was I dead? No, I couldn't be dead, could I? No, I am not dead because I am thinking. You can't think when you are dead, right? Wow something was digging into my lower back and it hurt, a lot! Wait, it was digging into my wrists, and they were behind my back. Aw crap, it's my handcuffs, they are what is digging into my wrists, and they are stuck behind my back. This is entirely not a good place to be in. Suddenly, as if a heavy fog was lifted, I could see again when the blindfold was removed. There he was, and unbelievably so, standing in front of me as I sat tied to one of the folding chairs in the room. "Holy shit, how are you here right now?" I growled.

"That is the first question you have for me? I should think you might like to know who I am first." He snarled back at me. "My name is Hector, you dipshit, and you owe me a car, and I think I will take yours along with a few of the items you have in here as a bonus tip for my troubles." There is a point in time where the stress of life, or just general situational stress, can get the better of someone. I'd like to think, looking back, that this was the point in time where it got the better of me, and rightly so. I looked up at Hector and just started laughing. This wasn't your normal laugh though; it came from deep down inside me and sounded nothing like a response to comedy. It was evil, and I never want to hear it again. The blood was oozing now, down over my face and I must have been a sight for the comic books. Bloody, battered, tied to a chair in full body armor, and laughing in the face of my own gun pointed at my head. I was surely losing it.

Hector had a look in his eyes that I was scaring him a little as he took a step back. I looked over at Phoebe who stood several feet away, and seemingly scared out of her mind, definitely enough to piss her pants. "Really, Phoebe?" I said scowling at her as she stood behind Hector, "All you had to do was point and shoot . . ."

Hector's eyes widened and the blood on my face from my own wounds was joined soon thereafter by the blood from Hector's. His head exploded, and I watched as his eyes recognized the horror that was destroying him before his body could react. The shower of blood, bone, and brain hit my face with such force that it felt like being sandblasted for a split second. His body fell forward onto me, knocking the chair I was strapped to over, and we all went down in one giant bloody mess. The floor was now bathed in a dark, syrupy red coat of blood and brain matter that looked to be spreading its wings out in all directions.

"Ugh! Get this asshole off of me, Phoebe! Help me up, this is disgusting!" I looked over at her, adjusting myself the best I could to see past the crater in Hector's disfigured head as it rested on my chest. Phoebe was frozen stiff, the gun still smoking in her hand. I can't believe Hector assumed she wasn't armed, what an idiot! Oh, and how thankful I was, at the same time, for taking the chance on Phoebe and giving her a gun.

"Phoebe, Phoebe!" She wasn't checking in. "Phoebe!" I yelled. "Get a move on it, there were three of them remember! Let's go, Phoebe, please help me up. The keys to the cuffs are in my right front pocket. Come on, girl, you need to start moving. Now! Move now, Phoebe! Come on, Phoebe, I can't do this without you!" She false-started a couple times and then set her gun down on the ground before vomiting uncontrollably all over the floor in front of her. She rocked a little on all fours while crying and spitting the remnants of her breakfast out of her mouth. I just looked at her, watching the realization of what she had done wash over her like a mudslide. I had read about this once, and talked to some friends who had seen combat. The body's reaction to killing can sometimes get the better of someone. I didn't know what to say just then, wondering if sarcasm might be the best route to take. So I went for it, "That's it Phoebe, get it out now since there is already a mess on the floor from Hector's current leaking issue."

She glared at me, trembling after her ordeal, and wiped her mouth with the back of her hand. She then made her way over to me, crawling around the growing mix of blood and vomit on the floor. While crouching, she grabbed Hector's feet and dragged him away from me. She then reached into my pocket, got the key and unlocked my cuffs. From there I told her to go sit in the truck and I would do the rest. She did not argue. I made sure she left her gun, that way she couldn't entertain any thoughts of suicide after taking another human being's life. Regardless of the fact that he probably and most likely was going to kill me, killing another human being is not an easy or natural thing to do. There are times the reaction to the act can be even as drastic and just as permanent as the act itself. More often though, the act leaves huge, emotionally deep psychiatric scars, that will forever haunt the responsible.

I quickly rounded up my weapons, making sure they were ready, and performed a quick survey of the surrounding area. The grounds at my level were clear so I went up to the roof and looked in all directions for any movement. I listened for several minutes and heard nothing but the wind and a few birds. Where were the other two guys I had seen before with Hector? Did he just not bring them with him? They had to be out there somewhere. I wasn't going to be fooled a second time. I still had the remnants of his skull on my face from the first and hopefully last big mistake I made today. I headed back down off the roof and went to work on cleaning out the storage unit and removing the body. I grabbed a shovel from the unit and dug a hole out behind the units big enough for Hector. Once I was satisfied no one would find his body anytime soon, I made sure all the blood was out of the unit and that the smell was replaced with bleach. Again, I stood back for the second time this morning and was happy with leaving the unit better than I had found it. It was now eleven in the morning, and we had gone nowhere.

I changed my clothes, still fancying the tan pants and black polo look I had on before, and cleaned myself up the best that I could. Disinfecting and cleaning my wounds would not be chalked up in the category of things I would like to repeat. Having a mirror in the unit made the ordeal a little less complicated. I bagged up the bloody clothes and remaining trash left over from our stay in the unit the night before, then headed to the door and threw the bags into the bed of my truck. I pulled the truck out and locked the unit back up. When I sat down in my truck I looked over at her for the first time since I sent her to sit in the truck in the first place. She looked just as I had expected, a blank expression on her face, her chin resting on her fist, her elbow on the door's edge, looking out the window at nothing in particular. She did not seem troubled or distraught, which meant nothing, but she did engage me when I asked her if she was ready. "Yeah, I am ready, I'd like that gun back when you feel comfortable with me having it again. I don't feel safe anymore without it." I smiled and shifted the truck into gear

We went through the gate and I stuffed the trash bags as far down into the dumpster out in front of the facility as I could and made haste for the road once back in the truck. Again, I didn't see a car, or person for that matter, in site. What the heck, where was everyone? I expected more chaos than this, anything but total silence. Something didn't feel right. Even before the events that are unfolding, there was more activity around this area than today.

"How do you think Hector found us?" she said, still facing out her side window. She turned to face me, adjusting herself in her seat and moved the seatbelt out from in front of her neck. "How in the heck did he find us, James? That doesn't make any sense at all." She was clearly upset now, she didn't show it, I could just tell by the tone in which the words came out of her mouth. "I am a normal person and I would not think to look where we were, nor did he have the chance to follow us. He already knew where the storage unit was, didn't he? Did you know him, James?"

"Good god, no I did not know him. Seriously? I think I know, though, how he found us and the more I think about it the more pissed I get." I looked over at her briefly and attempted to smile, yet failed. "In our group of 'ants' we have a brother, well, we have an associate that has issues with partying. He gets messed up and drunk and starts talking. He talks a lot, we found out, and tends to not keep secrets very well when he is high. Hector didn't seem like the most reputable of individuals, and I think he heard about our checkpoints and BOL from Trevor, our one and only weak link. The way I see it now, Hector's run-in with us was just some bizarre coincidence and nothing else. He was headed there already; he didn't know I was as well. If I hadn't run into you they might have gotten the better of me at the unit when I arrived." If I ever saw Trevor again I planned on showing him just how grateful I was for his big mouth. I knew we should never have let him in the group, but he was basically a brother to us, that's why we tolerated him.

The road was barren, two lanes going on forever through a valley with mountains on both sides. Any other day I might stop to take in the sights, but we were behind schedule now and running late. The sky, directly above us, was a bright blue color with a few scattered clouds. The horizon, however, in all directions, was a dark brown and black color from all the smoke.

"What do you suppose that is?" she asked pointing out her window. "That, over there, flying just above the mountain range. See it?"

I squinted as I strained to look across the dashboard out her side of the front window. What was that, a helicopter? It certainly wasn't one I had ever seen before. It sort of looked like a cobra attack helicopter; only this one appeared to blend in with the distant smoke and every so often would disappear completely. It suddenly banked in our direction and when doing so became very visible for a split second. It certainly was like no helicopter I had ever seen, and it was headed straight for us. I did not feel good about this. We were out in the open. I mean we were really out in the open, and I hadn't considered a threat from above as an issue at this point. I was more concerned with ground threats and crazy people; this scenario had not been played out in my head just yet.

I rolled down the windows a few inches to see if I could hear anything other than the wind. I couldn't, but we were traveling about 80 mph at this point, so that wasn't unexpected. The copter flattened out, still coming at us, and vanished from view again. Suddenly dirt and gravel flew in the window on Phoebe's side, along with metal and plastic from my truck. The pilot was firing at us with his onboard machine gun, for some reason. My truck's engine compartment was obliterated and we came to a slow and silent stop as steam and various other fluids spewed out of my truck. The helicopter flew by directly overhead and I knew he wanted a second pass at us and was positioning himself for just that. As it flew over, I realized I couldn't recognize anything about it. It displayed no writing, no symbols, and yet it still remained difficult to see, like it was phasing in and out of optical view. "Get out of the truck, Phoebe! Now! Head over to the side of the road and hide on the other side of the embankment, okay. Go, go now, Phoebe, and stay out of sight."

The pilot was preparing to finish his banking turn, coming around to finish me off as I was pulling out the AR-15. I turned on the red dot scope and brought it up to view, making my way around the truck to use as cover. The pilot leveled off, and I began firing three round bursts directly at him and his rotor, knowing full well they would most likely accomplish nothing; but I wasn't going to just sit here and take it. He returned fire; his rounds began to hit the dirt several yards ahead of me and ripped through the asphalt, lining up perfectly with me. While I continued to fire, my red dot failed. His rounds stopped prior to hitting my truck a second time, and he came into full view. Something catastrophically failed on his end as well, because whatever system he had on board that regulated the stealth technology he was using was no longer operating properly. I heard his rotors, for the first time also and his engine started to sputter. He fell out of the sky like a rock.

Yeah, he was falling out of the sky all right, directly at my truck with me standing behind it. "Shit!" I yelled as I leaned and dove out of the way. "Phoebe, lookout!" I screamed as I hit the ground rolling. His tail end smashed into the bed of my truck and his cockpit slammed into the roadway and went down the embankment in Phoebe's direction. The sound of metal fragmenting and tearing was grotesque. There was no fire or explosion that accompanied this crash, which was nothing like the movies. The helicopter rolled, twisted, and came to a violent stop about fifty yards from the road, having plowed a trail in the low-lying grass, leaving behind fresh dirt. I had come to a rest sitting on my ass, my legs out in front, leaning on my arms behind me, dumbfounded by what just happen. Surely it wasn't my shooting that did this. There is no way I am that lucky. Whatever caused this copter to fail might have caused my red dot to fail also. No matter, I will figure it out later. Where the hell was Phoebe?

I needed to do two things right now, make sure she was okay and check the crash site. The order in which those took place was important. The last thing I wanted to do was be caught helping Phoebe and get shot in the back. I pushed the inoperable red dot scope out of the way and used iron sights for the time being, till I could fix what was wrong with it. With my rifle raised, I moved towards the debris field, scanning the area for Phoebe. I also took a quick look around, no cars coming, no other threats in the air as far as I could tell and no one visible on foot. It was now just me and the damn pilot, and Phoebe, wherever she was. "Phoebe?" I called out as loudly as I could while trying to remain quiet. "Phoebe, where are you, dammit?" I panned around and couldn't see anything moving. Great, she was plastered to the bottom of the helicopter; that had to be where she was.

"I'm over here, James." She called out to me but I couldn't see her.

"Over where?" I asked.

"Over here, you jerk, are you trying to get me killed today?"

No way, I was dumbfounded in disbelief. She had found a storm drain that ran under the road and climbed into it. "You've got to be kidding me?" I was surprised at the joy in my voice. "Are you alright?" She crawled out and looked at me.

"Of course I am alright, I didn't think you were, though. Once you started shooting I thought that was it for both of us and jumped in here. What happened?"

I let my AR fall to my side and hang on the three-point sling I had. I helped her out of the storm drain and hugged her. "I'm okay, James, really I am. How are you though?" I let her go and stood back.

"I'm ok for now, but I need to go check the pilot and see if I can get some answers because this whole thing is bullshit. Do me a favor, head back up to the truck and pull the two backpacks out from behind the front seats. Okay? Those are for us. We are obviously on foot now. Anything else you think you can salvage, do it, and make a pile on the opposite side of the road from the crash site. I will be right back." She nodded at me and got to work heading back up the embankment to the road. I was proud of her, either she was just full of dumb luck or she was learning. Either way, it was nice to not be alone right now.

I turned around and began to make my way towards the downed copter. I made sure to give the crash a wide berth and approached from the driver side, if there was one, rifle up and ready. The helicopter came to rest right side up and the cockpit was facing away from me. I remember firing twelve rounds, four bursts, before the crash, so I had eighteen left to go. Plenty for this conversation; I had more strapped to my left thigh if need be. I didn't anticipate there being much of a conversation though. The cockpit window was torn off and the cab was open. I could see the body of the pilot sitting motionless in the compartment, his helmet still on. Once I had the upper hand in tactical positioning I picked up a rock and tossed it at the pilot. It landed on the passenger side ground and he raised his side arm, firing off a couple rounds in the direction of the noise. I picked up another rock and repeated the process, only this time he didn't fire at the sound, rather attempted to unbuckle his harness and get out of the cockpit. He cried out in agony, though, and stopped all attempts at getting out of his seat. He then, instead of trying to get out of his harness, pulled off his helmet and threw it out into the dry grass yelling something I didn't understand. "Do you speak English?" I said from the cover of the grass, hopefully out of his reach with that side arm.

He stopped moving and just stared forward, "Yes" he sighed, "I speak English." He settled back into his seat and I could see he held his sidearm flat against his chest. Well, he wasn't dumb.

"I am not going to hurt you, I want to talk to you." I remained where I was, minutes earlier he wanted to kill me; I wouldn't be forgetting that too easily.

"Well, talk then," he said, staring straight forward. His hair was cut short, from what I could tell, and looked like a military cut, all the edges were clean and he looked to be fit and in good health, other than his current injuries.

I realized I didn't know what to say now, I didn't really think this through entirely. "Uh, yeah, why in the hell did you shoot at me?" It certainly sounded better in my head.

He coughed a little and adjusted his harness. "My orders; they were to shoot anything that moves in this area. Primarily vehicles."

"Even non-military vehicles?" I asked. I was catching on to what he might be.

"Especially non-military vehicles. My orders were to disable any vehicles and remove any threats. You weren't a threat until you fired back at me."

I laughed. "Same goes for you, big guy. I hadn't planned on shooting at you until you destroyed my truck and almost killed me in the process. I would have been fine with simply admiring your helicopter from afar. Which, by the way, is my next question, why did you crash?"

This time he laughed. "Something knocked out all my electrical systems; I can assume that wasn't you, so it must have been someone else. All I know is that nothing works, no radio, no lights, no anything. What about you?"

The slogan, "Made in China" ran through my head as I peered over at my red dot and still maintained my aimed on him. "Yeah, kind of having the same issue myself." I looked over at the truck. From here I could not see her but I had a feeling she was ready. "What's your name?" I asked in his direction.

"My name? It is Duyi," he replied.

"Well Duyi, I'm James, do you want help out of the cockpit?" He hesitated and then threw his gun out in my direction.

"Yes, please, I am pretty stuck in here."

I called out to Phoebe and she peered over the truck at me. She gave me a thumbs up, and I waved her over. When she got to my side, I handed her the rifle and told her to stay put and cover me. She looked puzzled. "We can't just leave him there, so watch my back while I help him." She took the rifle and knelt in the grass. "Duyi, you try anything and my partner here is going to fill you so full of lead that you won't know which hole to take a shit out of, understand?" He said he understood and I slowly approached the copter.

"Put your hands up and keep them up Duyi, you move even a little bit and I will put a bullet in your head." I got to his side and looked in. He had bone sticking out of his right thigh and his left foot was sheared off. I made sure he didn't have any other weapons and holstered my handgun. I had him unbuckle his harness and put his left arm around my right shoulder. With one movement and a lot of noise from him I pulled him out and set him down on the ground next to his cockpit. From here the helicopter rotors provided enough shade to reduce the day's heat.

"Ugh, there is a med kit with some pain medication and field dressings attached to the back of my chair. Can you get that please?" I looked over at Phoebe; she still had the gun trained on Duyi so I took a look in the cab. All of the controls were in an Asian language I did not recognize. Duyi looked Chinese but I could be wrong; I wasn't very good at telling one Asian descent from another at times. I found the kit and brought it to him. He removed a syringe from the little kit and plunged it into his thigh. After removing the needle he leaned back and rested his head on the cockpit outer wall. He watched me with such detachment while I bandaged up his wounds that for a moment I thought he had passed out. He knew it as well as I did that he would die from these wounds without help; and we both knew help wasn't coming. I knelt down next to him and could see the glazed look of relief settling into his eyes, the medication was working and he relaxed a little. "Duyi, we are going to leave now. You can see your gun over there." I said pointing to it in the grass several yards away. "I am obviously not going to get it for you. I noticed the camel pack on your back so I won't get you any water. One last question before we go though." As I stood he looked up at me slowly, his head seeming to be heavy now. "You're the first wave of what country, Duyi?"

He just looked at me for several seconds and then smiled an almost drunken smile. "China, James, I am from the great country of China . . ." He said this with his arms held out wide and then dropping them to the ground, he fell silent. His head slowly dipped and his breathing calmed.

I smiled back at him. "Well, good luck with that Duyi, let's see if China comes and gets you." As I turned to walk away Phoebe handed me my rifle and I slung it over my shoulder fitting it into place once again.

"You too, James. China isn't the only one here now." I paused and turned to face him. He kept his head bowed, "Good luck to you too James, I am truly sorry, if that matters any." His laugh was distant, yet coarse and then he coughed a painful cough that made him groan and his head bob a little.

I turned my back to him and continued walking over to what was left of what was once my truck. I could hear him laughing still, softly to himself, the meds obviously doing their job to help him ignore the pain. I remember actually feeling bad for him as I looked at my truck. It would have been so much easier to hate him if I never talked to him. I would have to remember how this made me feel and not do it again if the chance arose. Otherwise, I would never make it in this new world and would let my family down by not seeing them once more, and seeing them whole.

Phoebe was silent behind me as I took in the scene, standing several paces away. No sound except the wind could be heard as it blew softly past us. Any other day I might pull out a chair and a beer and enjoy this moment. Turning around to face the helicopter, I could still see Duyi's legs as he sat there. If I took a couple steps to the left I would be able see him in full view, yet I opted out of doing that. It was hard enough already, for some reason, to leave him there; the last thing I needed to do was continually look back and be reminded of it. I turned around and walked past my truck and down the embankment on the other side where Phoebe had put the supplies. She had done a pretty good job of getting the things we needed out of the truck on her own. Yet, I still needed to make sure we had everything that was of use to us now. I looked over at her and we made eye contact, she smiled at me and twisted her right hip in my direction showing me that she had returned the revolver to its rightful place in her holster. She must have seen me put it in the center console when we left the storage unit earlier.

I smiled in her direction and told her that I was going to look through the cab once more before we got moving. As I started going through the truck cab area, I found the sealed map package my brothers and I had made tucked under the driver's seat, and I could hear Phoebe milling about outside. Along with the maps I found the list of locations around the BOL that could be temporary safe havens if we found ourselves in need of one. Mainly, the list included towns and what was in those towns regarding shops and hotels. The tent and sleeping bags we had could hopefully prevent us from having to go into town, but I wasn't sure now how long the food and water would last us. Looking at the map, I figured we had something like a hundred and fifty to a hundred and eighty miles left to go to the second checkpoint. Ugh, that was discouraging I thought and kept that to myself. Phoebe had enough on her mind now and didn't need anything like that to think about. I looked around for road signs or anything else that may help me make a better estimate of where we were. There was nothing to be seen though, and if we waited around any longer, I anticipated more attention might make its way here.

I finished my inspection of the cab and returned to where Phoebe was. She had her backpack on and looked as ready as she ever would be, prompting me to do the same. As I put my backpack on I placed the maps in the front pocket of my vest. The vest was heavy and felt even heavier with the pack now hanging on it; however, it still felt really good to be wearing it. If we paced ourselves I had no doubt I would be able to manage the extra weight. Once I was ready I pulled the map back out and showed Phoebe which direction we needed to go, emphasizing the route of travel being away from the roads. She was quick with her response; pointing out the obvious hindrance that taking the route I chose would be more difficult and take much longer. I just gave her a look. I think it was enough of a look that didn't require me to say that regardless of the fact that it was a more difficult route, it was a safer route.

I put the map away again and took in a deep breath, sighing silently. I looked down at my feet as I took that first step forward, thinking to myself that this was going to be uncharted waters for me, surely Phoebe as well. I kind of felt like an explorer, of sorts, that took those first steps into the unknown, or that first step off the ladder onto the surface of the moon. The math started rolling through my head, and as it did my heart became heavy. We had something in the way of around four hundred miles to the BOL. Normally that figure wouldn't be so daunting, having a vehicle to use, and would take the better portion of a day to complete. Moving at a steady, hopeful pace of twenty-five miles a day on foot put the time range in somewhere around two to three weeks, give or take a couple days. A week, at best, was the time needed to make it to the second checkpoint. We had enough water for a few days and would need more before getting to the next storage unit; yet our food supply was not an issue. The math began to fade the more I thought about it. Having put things into a better perspective, I didn't feel so bad about how far we had to go now. The only thing I would continue to worry about would be our safety in the world around us. Outside of the truck we had a lot more to consider. The last thing we needed now was to be careless and break an ankle misjudging a step.

My mind drifted back to reality when the sound of the leaves and dry grass began to crack under our footsteps as we trudged onward. Looking over my shoulder I estimated we had gone about a thousand yards already, the smoldering wrecks of the truck and helicopter becoming harder and harder to see without something like binoculars to assist our vision. We soon reached the base of the hills I had seen from afar. They, for the most part, retained the foliage that the grassy valley possessed for several hundred yards up into elevation. I could see that when we reached the top of the first hill we would begin to traverse a new kind of topography. Trees could be seen littered among the hills off in the distance, and if I was honest with myself, I could not wait until we reached them. Something had to be said for the feeling of walking through a forest, or at the very least, a grove of trees. It was like you were among the old and the very wise. When I was younger and heard that there were living things that had been around much longer than I was or ever would be, it fascinated me. The thought of a turtle living upwards of a hundred plus years is just amazing.

Growing up, we had a neighbor that lived on our street, an older lady, perhaps in her late nineties when I was young. She later would pass away at the age of a hundred and three, but I never would forget how I felt when I heard the year in which she was born. My dad told me after I brought over some freshly picked tomatoes to give to her from our garden that she was born in the year 1899. Whenever I heard the year 1800 all I could think about were cowboys and the life of the old Wild West. How thrilling that must have been to grow up in a time like that and then live on to see three centuries. I never forgot the feeling I had when I was in a room with that woman. Her physical beauty in the eye of the world had faded long ago, yet the amount of wisdom and sheer life experience she beheld could fill a museum. It was apparent to even a not so observant bystander that this woman had a lot to offer, and if one was to take the time and listen they could gain so much from her. The years would pass and I would get older, losing sight of that childlike wonder with the world and would stop visiting her due to the "busyness" of life.

I remember when my parents told me she had died. I recall listening to the fact that she was found in her home, asleep in bed, having gone to sleep for the last time. The feeling that overcame me when I realized that she had done so alone stopped me cold. I never appreciated the fact that she, having been alone for a very long time before she died, had outlived almost everyone that she had ever loved. How selfish I had been as a kid, to not take the time each day to visit her and just say hi more than I did. I truly missed out on something that could have made me a better me. Instead, I had inadvertently chosen to face life on my own through selfishness and immaturity, passing on a world of wisdom living right next door. I never weighed in the magnitude of what I could have learned from her when I was younger until much later in life. It saddens me, even to this day, and I will forever pray she forgives me of my wrongdoing, leaving her alone in that house. Every time I see an aged tree, especially a grove of trees or a thick dense forest, I think of all those I have ever had in my life that were full of wisdom through a long life before me.

So now, as I gazed upon these hills and saw the thousands of trees, I stifled a quick prayer under my breath, begging for guidance, yearning for wisdom, that I may face the coming trials ahead of me.

Chapter 6

. . . Amongst the Stars . . .

We decided to set up camp later that evening, finding a quiet spot with good coverage. We kept from starting a campfire for several obvious reasons, but primarily because it wasn't needed. The wind died down as the sun was setting, and there wasn't a cloud in the sky. The temperature remained about the same once the darkness set in. Summer hadn't escaped us yet and, if I had it my way, hopefully wouldn't leave at all for the next month or so. The tent was backed up to a large rock with three trees forming a triangle pattern around it. As we passed by this spot earlier, I made a point to remember it, thinking at the time that it would provide a great place to set up camp. We continued on for several hundred more yards before I decided to backtrack and use that spot instead of continuing on in hopes of finding another. Phoebe had pretty much kept to herself during our hike. I think she sensed I had a lot on my mind and wasn't in the mood for chitchat. Even when I wanted to turn around, she just went along with the flow, having most likely seen the expression on my face.

Once we arrived back at the site where I wanted to set up camp, I made a note in my head to stop the next time I came across a good camping spot as the evening closed in. If I started to second-guess myself with the little things, I might make a huge mistake in the near future with something larger than a campsite choice. I really needed to listen to my gut feeling more, especially now, when it was starting to count for more than just the feeling of butterflies. An outdoor supply store I often frequented over the past couple of years, delivered the better portion of what made up our camp tonight. We each had a compact +10 degrees sleeping bag and a pillow to go with it. I decided to carry the tent that wasn't more than a couple pounds of weight and it went up with ease once I pulled it out. Having chosen the black colored tent and having to wait a few weeks while it was back ordered turned out to be a great decision on my part. If you walked away from camp, without a campfire, the tent was almost impossible to see up against the rock, even if you knew it was there and tried to look for it.

After camp was settled, I climbed up on top of the rock we set up next to so that I might be able to see what we were surrounded by. I told Phoebe what I was doing before I left and she soon joined me up there. We laid on our stomachs, heads barely popping up, maintaining a very small stature as to not silhouette our selves against the dimming night's sky. I could see her out of the corner of my eye trying to mimic my actions, taking into account what I was doing and figuring out why on her own. I felt her reaching out and she pressed the bump that had formed on the top of my head after Hector struck me there. I winced and pulled away, giving her a slight shove with my shoulder while trying to concentrate on the task at hand. "You need to clean that wound again, James." Without looking over at her, I acknowledged her observation with a nod.

Despite my best efforts I couldn't see much farther than a thousand yards in only a couple directions. I would need to find higher ground if I wanted to gather a better vantage point. For now though, I was able to see a long ways away in the direction we had come and, even though I couldn't see the road, the general direction of it was in view and showed signs of no movement or lights. Phoebe mumbled something to the degree that she was getting tired and would like to sleep. I told her I would stay up a while so that she could do just that, and I would keep watch. As we climbed down I helped her off the rock and she tightened her grip on my hand as I gave it to her for balance. She held on to it longer than one normally would and gave it a tight squeeze before she let go entirely. I couldn't help but smile at the gesture.

Watching her walk away I hadn't really thought much of it yet, but she had gone through a terrible ordeal with Hector. Regardless of whether anything happened or not, her last few days had been, more than likely, harder than she had ever experienced in her life thus far. Normally, I would have taken this into account and pondered the crap out of it over and over again in my head, but for some reason, today didn't give me that luxury. I tended to really over-think every thing I experienced, having an inability to let things go. This happened so much so that towards the end of each day I would find myself so wide-awake late into the night that falling asleep rarely was an option at that point. Tonight, however, I had completely disregarded the whole possibility that Phoebe had been raped before I found her, and I suddenly felt terrible about it. There were these moments in the past that I would be so overcome with emotion that I would have to stop and feverishly focus on something else just to get through it. If I didn't, the feelings would completely conquer me, causing me to then fall into a deep depression. I never understood it. Why I could be totally fine one moment and then the next be almost suicidal? Obviously, I never followed through with the feelings, but no one around me ever noticed these sudden changes in regards to my internal turmoil. I must have kept it under wraps well enough to never bring attention to it. There were times, however, that I wished those around me could hear me crying out for their help, dying ever so slowly and subtly within the recesses of my own mind.

More often I would ride out the emotions alone, carrying on as if nothing was happening until I had the chance to finally go to bed. Then I would dream unimaginable nightmares all night long, waking in a cold, drenched sweat, feeling scared and alone for several minutes before I was able to figure out they were just dreams. Then, I would get up, start my day usually before the sun had risen, and act as if nothing had happened, hoping that I might be spared that experience on this new day. This particular tribulation would persistently unveil itself, for the most part, daily in my life and once again it was happening now. When Phoebe let go, it all began to unfold in my head in a matter of seconds, and I stopped dead in my tracks. I needed to take a moment to calm the waters within myself. I could hear her as she stopped walking back to camp and turned to look at me. The moon was coming out and was only a faint sliver of its whole self, yet it shed enough light for us to see each other clearly in the dark.

I must have been a sight to see, staring at nothing in particular, hands clenched at my sides and taking a few deep breaths. I looked over at her and she cocked her head to one side ever so slowly as she appeared to analyze what I was doing and said, "I am sure we will talk about a lot of things as our time together lengthens, but right now I am tired so I am going to go to sleep. Will you be okay?" Looking at her I nodded and she continued back to camp, leaving me alone with my thoughts. The day was over and as the stars began to come out in the night sky it was difficult to reflect back upon the day's events. Duyi was most likely dead by now, and having met him changed the course of how I would perceive today's events and the events to come. I wish I had watched the helicopter explode into oblivion rather than crumble into a broken mess on the ground. I could have gone without ever meeting the pilot on a personal level. I know now, that any more interaction I have during this conflict with anyone else like Duyi will be that much more difficult to bear having a face to put on the enemy. In another time and place, I think I could have been friends with Duyi, perhaps even good friends, but not today.

This morning I had started out with an agenda of my own and a desire to be nothing more than a conscientious observer making my way home. The day's events, however, changed everything for me, forcing me into the role of active participant and critical decision maker. I already placed another human being in harm's way more than once, assisted in the killing of another, and watched the final moments of one man's life slip away. Is this what the world is really like? Have we separated ourselves so far from the close proximity in which life and death coexist that when they collide it is shocking to us? Or, am I the one that is separated from it all? I am beginning to wonder if my heart is in any of this, or that maybe it is not even participating in the production that is within me.

I know, all too well, that what I am going through right now, sitting on this rock, watching the horizon, is something I have been going through for as long as I can remember. Sometimes I cry out from within, hoping that someone will hear me and save me from this inner turmoil. Mostly though, it goes unheard and unnoticed. I am left with the daunting task of facing all of this on my own, forever weighed down by my own fears, heartaches, and relentless self-hatred. There are times, even now, that I will lie in bed after a day's activities and wonder what it was I actually did that day that was worth anything to anyone. Did I do something that perhaps might make the world a better place? Or did I just waste away another day, leaving it behind me to rot like the rest. I think the last two years of my life have been the most fulfilling. Having spent it entirely preparing for a future I thought would be exciting, and now being surrounded by it, I am forced to see that I never truly wanted to find myself in this predicament. I only wanted to find something worthwhile to do with my life, something to take my mind off of the losses and set my eyes on the possible gains. I need to find another reason to keep going, something that can replace the strength of a lost love and something that isn't ephemeral or short lived.

My motivation, at one time, was to keep pressing forward in a hope to see my old girlfriend again some day. I know to some, that kind of motivation can seem fleeting, even childish. But, to those that can relate, it can be the most pressing motivation one can find within themselves. As time has faded though, and I have heard from her less and less, my desire to press on has broken down. There were times that I wished for a quick end to this life I lead, one that would relieve me of the emotional storm within myself. Of course, I would never allow that to happen, primarily for one reason and one reason only. There was no way in hell I would ever go out easily like that. The thought of leaving this world quietly is more than frightening, even more so than facing my internal turmoil alone. I would rather not leave this world so easily; it is going to take a lot more than that. Momentary weakness on my part is something I face on a strictly theoretical plane, never a reality. The curiosity for tomorrow always outweighs the suffering of today, I figured. But if I had to choose, I would go out the same way I came in, bloody, naked, and screaming. That thought always makes me laugh.

The air was cooling and caused the wound on my forehead to ache. I reached up to rub it and winced when my gloves made contact. I needed to put some more disinfectant on it before it gets out of hand. I don't know what prompted the thought, but I suddenly remembered something. Before I left the hotel yesterday I sent out the text to our three control stations set up at both checkpoints and the BOL. I had forgotten to check the readings at the first checkpoint and scolded myself for that. The printout record would have been available on the receiver, regardless if we had power or not, and would have given me a rundown on everyone's status. I had not given it a second thought, figuring we would have made it to the BOL by now. It would have been nice to know where everyone was and, perhaps, if I would be running into any of them in the near future.

I decided to climb down off the boulder and head back around to the tent. Phoebe was already tucked away inside, the zipper shut tightly allowing for no ability to peak in and check on her. I found my backpack and rummaged through till I located the antibacterial ointment. Removing a disinfectant wipe, I began to rub and squeeze the wound on my head until it bled again. Once the bleeding was stopped I applied the ointment and a new bandage. It always felt immediately better to relieve swelling from an infection, something one never forgets. I found a nearby rock and sat down, setting my pack next to me. I had a small cleaning kit for my gun in the outside pocket and pulled that out, setting it on my thigh and removing my gun from my holster. My rifle was leaning up against a nearby tree, and I glanced over at it as I disassembled my handgun. At that very moment the sensation of having only one shoe on overwhelmed me. It's kind of funny but that is how I felt, like if I had to run I would hobble with only one shoe, compared to having only one gun to fight with. These feelings I was having lately, new and fresh, were getting out of hand. I needed to realize, as much as one can prepare, that one can never be fully prepared and can only plan accordingly. I needed to clean my gun, and it needed to always be ready, but having it disassembled in front of me created a sense of unrest, like I was only half ready. Even though I could reassemble it in seconds, it still was an unsettling feeling, being alone out here under the stars.

Just then Phoebe coughed inside the tent, and I could hear her rolling over to get comfortable. Okay, I thought, maybe I am not completely alone and with that I went to work cleaning and oiling my gun. Once I was finished, I loaded it and placed it securely back in its holster. I then went to work on the rifle, repeating the process and reloading it as well. I then flossed my teeth, brushed them the best I could, and drank some water. Protein always seemed to keep me awake the best so I kept some beef jerky close by, as well as the floss since it always got stuck in my teeth. The hours streamed by and before I knew it Phoebe was tapping me on my shoulder after finding me dozed off. "Ugh, that was a mistake, I am sorry about that. What time is it, it's still dark?" I groaned out. She looked down at me as she stretched and said it was around five am and my turn to try and rest a few hours.

I stood up and stretched as well. I felt fine, reluctant to tell her I felt well rested, but I could tell she saw that I was. "We are going to have to work on this 'guard duty' stuff if either of us is going to try and stay up alone," she said. I looked over at her and could see her smiling at me in a sort of shitty way, and I just rolled my eyes and agreed.

I got to work on packing up the tent and sleeping bags while she pulled out some MREs for breakfast. Once the backpacks were packed, we sat together on top of the boulder and ate breakfast, neither one of us speaking much. I was beginning to really enjoy her company, despite my previous desire to have traveled this trip alone. The sun was starting to show itself behind the mountains off in the distance, and the birds could be heard as they bustled about in the surrounding trees. Besides the birds, there wasn't much of anything in the way of noise. The wind was non-existent, and with no cars around the morning was eerily silent.

This silence made it all the easier to hear the convoy when we did. Phoebe says she saw them first, but I disagree. In the direction of where the helicopter crashed and the remnants of my truck were, we could just make out the noise of at least a half dozen trucks on the road. I pulled out the binoculars I had in the bag and told Phoebe to take some cover. We laid flat on the rock and watched as a line of Humvees, we counted six as we passed the binoculars back and forth, moved on the road. They were heading in the direction we had been heading, and from the looks of it, pretty fast. After several minutes they were completely out of view and it was several more minutes before we could no longer hear them. Once we were convinced they were not coming back, we decided to pack up and start moving; as it happened, we would be heading in the same general direction they were. Things were getting a little interesting now.

Chapter 7

. . . Where Have All the Heroes Gone? . . .

I could see her walking up ahead of me, the holster on her hip flexing ever so lightly as she took each step. The handle of her revolver would move with the holster and swing outward as well with each movement of her thigh. She looked back at me and caught me looking at her 'holster' and just smirked. "I was looking at your gun, don't get any ideas," I said defensively in regards to the look she gave me. She turned back to the path ahead of her and replied without looking back at me.

"A man with nothing to hide needs no excuse." Well, she had me there, nothing too worthwhile to say in reply to that. Plus, I think if I did reply she would just shoot that down with another one of her proverbs.

Having spent the last five minutes or so taking in our surroundings as we walked, I was able to surmise that we had traveled around twenty to twenty-five miles from the crash site since last evening and were making good time. I figured in a day's travel we could, at best, put thirty miles under our belts. The average person can walk about three miles an hour, and given our combined health and load, we could accomplish this without any issues. With about twelve hours of good daylight available to use, we could easily accomplish thirty miles in a day. We had about three hundred and twenty-five miles to go till the BOL, another hundred and twenty-five or so till the next checkpoint. The only issue with any of this would be the terrain and any possible human contact we might find. I would like to go the whole rest of the trek to the next checkpoint and not see another soul. That, I figured, would be very unlikely; and, as if by some act of God, the thought triggered our current reality and Phoebe stopped dead in her tracks. She moved to cover herself with a tree signaling me to join her. I raced up to her while slinging my rifle forward. She began to kneel behind the tree that she had found as I was coming up right behind her to see what her alarm was about.

I really hated being right sometimes. I really, really, did. Several hundred yards ahead of us we could see a family moving through the brush. Phoebe pointed to the lead man, possibly the father of the family, out front with a rifle in hand. I could just make out three kids of various ages around ten years old, moving cautiously behind the man while two women were father back, both of them having rifles as well. All of them had several yards separating them from one another and were spread out over a thirty or forty yard radius. They had exited a grove of trees about a hundred yards prior and were almost through the open field in front of us. I told Phoebe to head perpendicular to our location away from the trail in an easterly direction, and I moved in the opposite direction to the west. I wanted to give this group a wide berth while they hopefully continued to head south between the two of us. With any luck they would narrow their course as they entered the woods where we were waiting, and move on by, never knowing we were here.

Phoebe and I had not discussed this scenario yet, much less any scenarios for that matter, and would have to handle this situation gingerly from the hip. I could see her ducking down behind a fallen tree and its leftover stump while I chose a rock to hide behind. We both dropped our packs and she readied her revolver while I posted up with the rifle. There was about thirty yards of distance between the two of us, hopefully leaving plenty of room for the group to pass through. As they approached, I silently prayed for the both of us. We were outgunned, yet had the advantage of location. I made sure that the spot I chose to hide in was offset from where Phoebe's was; that way I could try and avoid any crossfire. Still, the possibilities were endless and I had only taken into account a few of them.

I could hear the group approaching now, the kids making the majority of the noise, yet surprisingly less than would be expected. The man out in front broke the plain first and came into view. He was clean-cut, average build and height, with black short hair, looking to be in his mid thirties and Hispanic. He passed by the tree Phoebe had initially hid behind when calling to me to warn of the coming group. His sunglasses reflected the sun for a brief moment as he swiveled his head from side to side slowly and come to a stop. When he stopped he slowly knelt down and touched the ground around the tree. He then began to back up in a crouched position with his rifle out front, sweeping back and forth evaluating the surrounding area. He called to the ladies behind him to grab the kids and backtrack, using a few words I recognized from training with my brothers. Whoever he was, he was smart and aware. Granted, if we had wanted to get the upper hand on him he never would have seen it coming in time, but, regardless, he was observant and cautious. I liked that, however, at the same time I realized he wasn't to be taken lightly.

I could see the women corralling the children, two of which were little girls, and moving them a safe distance back into the field before ducking down and hiding in the grasses. The lone man took cover behind a tree and knelt down, waiting for the two women to get into position. The way they were acting troubled me. It was as if the world had changed overnight and that just didn't make sense. Or perhaps this guy knew more than most. It had only been three days since the bombings; I wonder how far out of the loop Phoebe and I had gotten. These people were paranoid and scared, yet driven enough to be overly cautious and very protecting of the children with them. The man was still in view of me and if need be, I had a perfect shot. He called out to us, "I know you are out there! Come out with your hands up! You have my word you will not be shot if you do!" I could tell he had done this before, yet he was uncomfortable with it this time. I think he knew more about us than he was letting on and, what we might be carrying.

I decided not to avoid him. Maybe he did know something that would help us. Either way, I was not coming out with my hands up; that's just stupid. "You have my word I won't shoot you, but I am not coming out with my hands up. Hold your fire I am coming out!" With that I stepped out from behind the rock with my rifle ready and gave him ample opportunity to size me up. Given the armor I was wearing and the fashion in which I was wearing everything else, he declined to push the issue further. He kept his gun ready, yet pointed it away from my direction, as did I, pointing mine away from him, and began my descent down the small ridgeline towards him. Once I came within ten yards of where he stood I stopped and introduced myself. He told me his name was Shane Thompson and that he was a Sherriff Deputy from a couple counties over. His story sounded very similar to mine and he made it as vague as possible which was nice, last thing I need to do is explain why I am being vague as well.

I glanced over at his remaining party members in the field while he explained their association to him. One woman was his wife and the boy was his son. The other three were his wife's friends that were over at their house at the time they left. He shrugged and just said he could not leave them behind. He gestured toward Phoebe's direction with his shoulder asking who she was. I gathered he had some experience tracking, based solely on the fact he knew that Phoebe was a girl. He smiled and said it was either a girl or a very light-footed petite male, and we both laughed a little. We exchanged information for the next five or ten minutes, the time kind of getting away from us. He was a good man, no doubt about it, just trying to make the best of a poor situation and keep his family safe at the same time. From the sounds of it their car shut off right around the time I had the incident with the helicopter, and they have been walking ever since. The children were traveling light, yet the grownups had bigger packs and seemed to be well fed and hydrated.

Soon enough the time came for us to get moving, and I called out to Phoebe to join me. She was reluctant at first, yet soon she was on my tail and Shane stepped aside to let us pass. We never shook hands, yet nodded in each other's direction, and I wished him and his family good luck. Shane said he hoped God would be with us, and Phoebe wished him the same for him and his family; I decided to just smile and keep my feelings about God to myself. As we stepped into the field, the two women stood up and watched us walk past keeping their guns to their sides. We gave them a good chunk of land for space as we made our way across the field. I said hello as we passed yet they all just watched us walk by, remaining silent. One of the little girls waved at us and was quickly scolded by her mother. Once we were to the other side of the field they too moved onward, seeming to try and catch up quickly to Shane who still stood at the edge of the forest watching us depart. I waved to him, and he waved back as they disappeared into the tree line.

Phoebe wanted to know what Shane and I had discussed, and I reassured her it was nothing she didn't already know but that when we made camp for the night I would fill her in. For the meantime, however, I wanted to concentrate on the path ahead of us and not bring attention to ourselves through idle chitchat. I think she got the idea because she no longer pressed the issue, rather fell into rhythm about twenty feet or so behind me as we pressed on. The rest of the hike was uneventful, and we made camp in a small grove of trees pressed up against the base of one of the many hills. A couple trees had fallen down and provided some good cover for a fire, which she and I started fairly quickly after we finished setting up camp. The fire was kept small, yet provided enough warmth and ease to allow a little bit of relaxation, something I had almost forgotten the feel of these past few days.

Before we would start our watches we would put the fire out, but it was nice to have it for a little while. Starting the fire was simpler than I had anticipated having matches on hand as well as a lighter. I can only imagine how much of a pain in the ass it would have been otherwise and was very thankful it hadn't gotten too cold and wet this year, even though we were approaching the winter season. As the sun set on another day it was becoming easier and easier to fall into this pattern. We still had plenty of food and water, yet finding a stream or river soon would be helpful. The map I had with us showed a river coming up soon, perhaps another day's hike and we would find it. Until then, the normal course we were taking was working out nicely.

Phoebe took first watch this evening, and I tried my best to sleep. There was no denying the fact I was tired, yet for some reason I had been having difficulty sleeping the past few nights.

Too much was on my mind, I figured, nothing that would be unexpected; however, it was becoming a hindrance, and if I didn't put an end to it soon, I would slowly become a wreck and unable to function. I knew all this, but could not change how it was playing out. I was worrying too much and needed to let a lot of it go. I think I was just so afraid that if I let my guard down in any way whatsoever, that in turn that would be my final mistake, resulting in either Phoebe or me getting hurt. I could hear her outside the tent, walking softly around camp and then finally settling on a nearby log. It was comforting having her here. Something about her set my restlessness at ease, as if peace just spread outward from her in all directions and permeated everything in its path, including me. The last thought I recall having that night was how she looked when I found her, helpless lying in the road, my lights flooding the darkening sky in all directions. I saved her, if only she knew how much she was saving me now, not leaving me alone and not letting me carry all this weight on my own.

The tent zipper slowly flipped open, and I could hear her calling out to me quietly and tapping my feet. "What time is it? Is it my turn to keep watch?" I asked as I strained to hear her speak; she was talking very quietly and I had to stop moving about so that I could hear her.

"It doesn't matter, James, you need to see this, come out here."

I threw off the sleeping bag and pulled my shirt over my head. Exiting the tent, I could hear it before I saw it. Rapid gunfire was very apparent off in the distance, followed by flashes of light that lit up the night sky over the chaos that was ensuing several miles away. Every so often an explosion would sound off, followed by more gunfire. Even if there were human cries amongst the activity, the splintering noise of warfare drowned them out.

The commotion was still a ways away and looked to have no intention of heading our direction, but it wouldn't hurt to be ready in case it did. I looked over at Phoebe and shrugged, "I have been asleep for, what now, four hours?" I estimated after looking at my watch, "How about you get some rest next? I will clean our guns and stay up the rest of the night. I feel fine anyways. Sound good?" She looked at over at me, her eyes reflected the light coming from the action off in the distance. A few fireballs rose into the air and lit up the surrounding valley where the conflict was taking place. I could also see a few buildings with each explosion as they became visible in the light.

"I really don't think I can sleep right now," she replied. "I feel fine as well. How about you show me how to clean my gun, and when I feel a little more comfortable with sleeping, I will try again?"

The moon was still only a sliver of itself, but bright enough to give well adjusted eyes enough light to move their owner around out here in the brush with ease. We sat together on the ground outside the tent, using the downed trees as cover, and I showed her how to dismantle her revolver, how to unload and reload it, and then how to properly clean and oil it. It did not take much to keep her engaged in the task at hand, which was nice. The last thing I want to do or enjoy doing is repeating myself. After we were finished with hers, I set to work on the rifle. She then reminded me about my meeting with Shane and wanted to hear about it. A part of me did not want to really relive that conversation because it was much more troubling than I had let on. Maybe it would be better for me to just talk about it with her and get it off my mind, rather than keep it in and let it eat me up. I looked over at her and could see the moon's reflection in her eyes. This picture was breathtaking by itself, add in the crisp air, the distant firefight, and the solidarity of our situation, one could find every emotion present.

I told her about how Shane had witnessed several bombings take place in his town while he was on duty. Soon after, the air raids picked up and the resulting destruction was immense. He was assigned to the local county SWAT team and before they could be deployed their operational headquarters was destroyed along with the majority of the law enforcement force preparing to head out. Agencies in the surrounding towns were having the same issues. The only officers that were left were the ones off duty and the ones out on patrol at the time of the bombings. Having no base of operations and communications being down helped in no way to reorganize the effort. Subsequently, everything went downhill from there. Any off-duty officers either lived too far away to respond quickly enough to help or decided it was better to take care of their families instead of coming in for a paycheck that most likely now, would never come. Shane was one of the lucky officers out on patrol when all hell broke loose. After finding out most of his force had been destroyed in the explosions and having no way to communicate with anyone else out in the field, he decided to head home and make sure his family was okay.

One thing led to another and after their car broke down while trying to head to a relative's place, they decided to finish the trip on foot. Running into us was one of many instances that they already had, ours happened to be the most peaceful one yet. I set down the rifle I was working on when I was finished and Phoebe took that as a chance to try and get some sleep. She headed to the tent without saying a word, appearing to be lost in her own thoughts. Saying goodnight as she slipped inside the tent wasn't beyond her at the moment, and then I didn't hear her move much after that. I sat there under the stars for some time, cleaning my sidearm before I got up to go take a piss. As I walked to find a nearby tree, from inside the tent Phoebe asked that I not go too far. I reassured her that she would still be able to hear me. "Don't worry I will aim for a rock so it makes some noise." I said as I chuckled a little bit.

"Don't be foul, James. It doesn't hurt to be a constant gentleman in the presence of a lady." I kept walking and just waved a hand at that, knowing full well that I have been nothing but a gentleman to her.

It is always easier to be an asshole to others instead of the good guy. My older brother always made sure we understood that we were the good guys, and always would be, regardless of what happened. My father did the job of instilling those beliefs in my oldest brother before any of us were born, my oldest brother being several years older than the next brother in line. However the world played out now, none of us would lower our standards and take advantage of those around us, even if we were starving and desperate. To go out like a man, with honor, that was our desire, and there was no other alternative for us. I believed that with all my heart. It is easier to be the villain, obviously, yet it is much harder to be the hero. The everlasting struggle of the good man to rise above the rest and lead by example is definitely not sought after by most, usually because it is much too difficult and reaps little reward in this life. My brothers and I would not be the ones to lose sight of that narrow path, it was ours to shoulder and carry. It was ours for the taking.

Chapter 8

. . . A Gentleman and an Officer . . .

Two more days went by, much like the first few and on the sixth day that Phoebe and I were together we found ourselves getting closer and closer to civilization. After a while it became difficult to avoid buildings and property owned by someone other than the state. Soon enough we hunkered down on one side of a small dirt mound and watched a group of people working on a few cars in someone's large backyard about a hundred yards or so away. These people never even noticed us, remaining busy with whatever it was they were doing. Every inch of my being wanted to remain hidden until nightfall and avoid any chance of being seen before moving forward. Phoebe, however, insisted we keep moving, further adding that she had a bad feeling about waiting here much longer.

Something about the people working on the cars bothered me though. All seven of them were male, save for one female in the bunch. Four of them were spread out evenly around the building in which they were working on the cars, and each of these four individuals was armed with a rifle. I could not tell any more details because of our distance from them except that they all had black hair and were of average height. I hated this just as much as Phoebe, but we had about thirty more miles to go until the second checkpoint. If we decided to avoid the coming town, the distance would double. I turned around, away from the group working on the cars and leaned up against the dirt mound, giving myself some time to think. Phoebe joined me, and I could tell she was looking at me, waiting to see what I wanted to do.

I could hear the group talking to each other, but they were too far away to clearly make out anything they were saying. One of the car hoods shut, then a second, and then a third. Soon the engines were coming to life, and I was beginning to feel a bit relieved. Maybe this group would leave, drive away from here, and we could pass on by undetected. I looked over at Phoebe and was about to smile and say we could wait it out for a second when something changed my mind. Instead of smiling at her I grabbed her head and pushed her into the dirt mound, followed shortly thereafter by piling myself on top of her as some kind of rocket coming in our direction was shot over us towards the group working on the cars. What followed was an amazing display of powerful pressure versus unknowing weakness. I never once decided to raise my head.

All I could do was listen to the carnage. Gunfire was all around us, coming in from one direction and heading out from another. It sounded like a hive of bees had been let loose above us as the bullets whizzed by. There was nothing I could do. If I raised my head even a few inches it would surely be blown off. I could hear shouts and commands coming from both sides, and despite the obvious firepower difference, both sides seemed equally trained and capable. There was no screaming or wild noises to be heard; instead there were instructions, orders, and tactics playing out on either side. Despite my better judgment, I decided to take a peak while Phoebe remained busy burying herself in the dirt. I opened my eyes to see a tan humvee, much like the ones we had seen the other day. This humvee remained still, idling on the main road about fifty yards away. This main road passed by the driveway that led up to the buildings nearby where the cars were being worked on.

On top of that tan humvee sat a machine gun manned by a soldier standing inside the cab with his upper torso protruding out of the roof. That gun let loose such an awful, constant barrage of fury that one would believe anyone at the other end of it would be indistinguishable from the surrounding topography after a few seconds. Meanwhile, two other humvees were moving around the main hummer and heading up the smaller road that headed to the location of the group working on the cars. As they were advancing, the main hummer continued letting loose its incredible onslaught of gunfire down range at the three cars. A couple soldiers had exited the firing hummer and were laying down their own fire, using the surrounding terrain as cover.

The two soldiers on the ground made eye contact with me and started heading our way, advancing in turn, giving each other cover as they moved toward us. One soldier, the lead, kept his gun trained on me while the other covered. Once near us they knelt down and asked us to identify ourselves, weapons still trained in our direction. The main humvee ceased firing and started to advance off road in the direction of the rest of their convoy. Silence settled on the surrounding area and the soldiers were able to lower their voices when they spoke to us. "Who are you?" the lead soldier asked. "What are you doing here?"

I started to sit up and he encouraged me to remain hunkered down. I looked at him and he just smiled back at me, "My name is James, this here is Phoebe." She decided to come out from her hole in the ground and meet our new friends. "We were trying to cross this field when all this started happening," I said as I waved my finger around in the air. "Who are you guys?" I tried to sound nonchalant as I asked, but it was hard to hide the fact that I knew who they were. He received an all-clear status from the humvees and stood to his feet, stretching out a hand in our direction, his partner doing the same. They helped us up and we brushed ourselves off. I turned around first while Phoebe seemed to want to delay that action as long as possible.

Behind us lay the remains of the group working on the cars. The soldiers were busy moving the bodies to a central location and searching them. Two of the cars were on fire; the third had more holes in it than I could count. "My name is Stevens, this here is Rochester. Our unit is out of Camp Pendleton, down south." He looked at me while he talked, Rochester kept an eye on the area. The main humvee drove past us while the gunner surveyed the area; the driver watched us as he passed by.

I looked back at Stevens after taking it all in and took a deep breath. "It is a pleasure to meet you both, thanks for the help," I said as I tipped the bill of my cap and smiled.

Stevens just smirked at me and started to walk away. "I hope you know how to use that rifle, we may be needing your help soon, we are a couple men short." Stevens said this over his shoulder as he headed over to the activity near the buildings.

Phoebe looked at me, appearing speechless, her mouth slightly open unable to say much of anything. "You mind repeating that please?" I asked confusingly. Stevens chose not to; instead he gestured for me to join him at the other humvees.

Phoebe grabbed my arm while I was contemplating the request. "I don't think this is a very good idea." Her grip tightened as she spoke, adding emphasis to her words. "This is not what we need to be doing right now." She was right, but maybe they could give us a lift the last thirty miles or so to the second checkpoint. That would really be a big help presently, considering that my feet were now raw and the rest of our trek headed through more urban type areas.

"We have about thirty more or so miles left to go, Phoebe. Right now their help is exactly what we need." An entourage, however, would make things either a lot easier or incredibly more difficult; either way, I wasn't sure at this point if I would have a choice in the matter.

As if reading my mind, Stevens pulled out a map of the region and unfolded it on the hood of the main humvee that was now parked. The gunner still stood at ready on top, headphones on and sunglasses glistening, periodically shifting positions to maintain visibility of the surrounding area. Rochester headed over to help the other soldiers and disappeared into the pack busying themselves. Phoebe reluctantly had followed me and now stood by my side, and rather closely I might add. Stevens tapped the map with his finger as he spoke, "Where is it you are headed, James? More than likely it is to a checkpoint, because you are much too close to civilization for it to be your BOL."

My jaw dropped and he leered at me with an obviously apparent shit-eating grin. His fellow soldiers weren't interested in our conversation as of yet and were still busy milling about. For now, it was just him and me. "You don't recognize me do you, James? I sure as hell recognized you and did so the second I saw your outfit and that patch on your arm. You are Eddy's little brother, the writer. Right? And most likely you are heading north to the BOL."

A long pause ensued after he spoke, longer than I would have liked to allow. This give him no other reason than to confidently feel he was right about what he had said. I felt my eyes narrow as I looked at him while I sized him up and tried to recall who he was at the same time. "Look, James, I don't mean any offense by any of this, we are just talking here. Plus, the way I see it, I had my chance to join you guys and I chose not to. Shame on me, right? Especially now."

I looked around again, contemplating what he was saying and wondering how in the hell our paths crossed like this. "I am sorry, Stevens, I don't remember you. There were a lot of people my brothers talked to who turned us down. That was something we had expected from the start. Our goals would appear crazy to most, while a waste of time to many more. Only a few thought it was wise." He looked solemn now, his eyes hid nothing anymore and I could tell his internal grief was getting the better of him.

"I wish I had taken your brother seriously. If I had, I might have the luxury of knowing my wife and kids are okay. Instead I have spent the last week or so in the dark, praying they are safe and not knowing anything about them or the rest of our family."

Things started to quiet down around us and the other soldiers were making their way to where we were. As the crowd thickened, the hair on my neck started to stiffen. I did not like being outnumbered and outgunned at the same time by people I couldn't fully trust. It really made me uncomfortable with just breathing the same air as they were. "James, where is it that you need to go? Show me." Stevens was tapping the map in front of him while the other soldiers were either eating, reloading, pissing, or watching us while possibly doing one or a few of the prior mentioned things. "I would be willing to take you there if you wouldn't mind lending us a hand in the meantime." His shit-eating grin returned. "The quicker I get all of this finished the sooner I can get back to my family; hell, the sooner we can all get back to our families." A few grunts and groans could be heard sounding off around the group, yet not a single one of them seemed to believe they would ever actually get home.

I reluctantly pointed to the town on the map at which the second checkpoint was located. "Now, what is it that I have to do to get Phoebe and myself there?" All I wanted to do was wipe that grin off his face, but for now I needed him. He looked down at the map, and then returned to me.

"Well, as you can see," gesturing over his shoulder, "we are becoming a bit short handed here and the possibility of reinforcements is slim to none." I took a look at what he was referring to and watched four marines, two of them injured, load two dead marines into the back of one of the humvees. "It's quickly becoming an 'all hands on deck' situation here, and if I didn't know any better I would venture to guess Eddy and the other brothers of yours trained you well. So I am sure you would be more of an asset to me than a hindrance, am I correct?" I wasn't about to begin lying at this point, so I just nodded at him, reluctant to offer up just how qualified I truly was.

"Very good then. Once we are finished here I will fill you in on what's going on when we get back on the road. There is another group, much like this one," he continued as he pointed to the fully grown pile of dead bodies near the burning cars, "that has been seen moving its way towards a small military ammo dump a few miles away from here. We have orders to stop them before they resupply. One of our convoys that started out ahead of us came under fire a few nights ago before we got to this area. Their assignment is now ours since we lost contact with them shortly after they came under attack. I'd like to head in the direction they went and maybe find some answers. Plus," pausing to shift his stance and readjust his sling so that his rifle rested under his right arm, he then slowly cracked his neck leaning it side to side before he continued to speak, "it just so happens we will be heading the way you need to go and can drop you off when we get there. It is your choice, James, but I highly recommend you get involved. This whole shit storm affects everyone. It is not like past incidents that took place thousands of miles away. This one," he emphasized pointing his finger downward, "is right in our backyard. So, get in, sit down, buckle up, and get on board for the big win, James. No sense in going at this alone."

With that he kept his shitty grin on high alert, opened the front passenger door of the main humvee and got in, closing the door behind him. I watched as he allowed his right arm to rest on the open window frame like someone getting ready to cruise the Sunday evening streets back home. I couldn't help but think that this guy had way too much confidence; either that or he was so battle weary that he just didn't care anymore.

Phoebe stood nearby and I could feel her gaze on me like a searing light bulb in a dark room. "Well, are you coming or not?"

I hadn't looked at her yet but I knew she heard me. Instead, I was busy watching the commotion around us.

The rest of the soldiers were loading up and one of them tossed a flare on the pile of dead bodies that was recently sprinkled with lighter fluid found in one of the nearby buildings. The pile erupted in flame, and puffs of thick black smoke began to rise into the air. "Let's move," bellowed Stephens from the front seat as he lazily waved an arm once in the direction he wanted to go, then he looked over in our direction and smiled. I opened the rear driver side door and seated myself inside looking over at Phoebe as I did.

"Do I have much of a choice in the matter?" she asked, hands resting on her hips.

I looked at her, smiling as I closed the door behind me. "No, not really. You might as well just trust me on this one, and my gut feeling hasn't let me down yet." I let my arm relax on the window frame as I sank into the comfortable seat. It had been only days since I left the comfort of my truck, but it felt like eons since I enjoyed the comfort of a good seat.

She reluctantly walked around to the passenger side, sat down next to me, and closed the door behind her. Before she could clamp down the seatbelt, the humvee roared to life and shot forward. Our driver positioned himself in the middle of the convoy, making sure he had one humvee in front and one in back of him. The gunners on all three vehicles kept busy surveying the area on all sides as we returned to the main road, heading north.

It was apparent already that we were heading towards where Stevens had wanted us to go, but I made a mental note to make sure it remained the direction I wanted to go as well. I didn't mind helping him out if he truly needed it, but I didn't want to become someone's scapegoat or bait in any matter. I also agreed with him that this was turning into a fight that needed to be fought by all, not just a few. However, my time to fight did not need to be right now, it would come later like we had all been planning it would. For now though, Stevens and his men were a means to an end that I did not want to pass up. Stevens put a headset on and signaled to us to put ours on as well. We picked them up from the side compartment in the door and once on, the outside noise dissipated, replaced by quiet static.

As Stevens spoke, I adjusted the volume with the knob on one of the earmuffs I was wearing; Phoebe did the same with hers. "So, I can tell you what I know, or I can tell you what I think is going on. You pick." I looked over at Phoebe and shrugged.

"How about a combination of the two, seems like it might be more interesting that way," I replied, reluctant to hearing dull facts on their own.

"Alrighty then, well, where to start I wonder? So I am sure you are aware of the several thousand well coordinated explosions that targeted government buildings, military installations, and communication facilities all across the country?"

It sounded like a rhetorical question, but I replied anyways, "Yeah, I know about some of the bombings, but nothing about the specific targets."

He didn't seem to take note of my reply and continued on with his story. "None of the targets were well populated ones, most were hit on lunch hours or picked when they were closed. The locations did cause a widespread overload of the emergency response system though and clogged every ability to fix the situations that kept unfolding all around us." He paused while watching a few burning buildings as we passed by them. They were fully involved with no one around, nothing we could have done even if we wanted to.

He adjusted himself in the seat and continued, "Only a few of the individuals performing the bombings have been found and have turned out to be anyone and everyone from religious nut jobs to retirees. There are turning out to be many, many pieces to this chess game, and the pawns are on the front lines as always while the ringleaders remain in the shadows. Anybody that the big puppet masters could get their hands on became assets. So far we have confirmations that some of the players are China, North Korea, a couple of the Mexican Cartels, Iran, and a few other smaller countries." He turned to look at me for a few seconds when he said the following; "I guess being the big kid on the block enabled everyone to want a piece of us after a while." Facing forward once more he pressed on, "All it took was a little planning and a lot of help to pull this off. It began with the bombings, followed closely behind with stealth bombing runs supported by several of the large players. Soon after the stealth issue became obvious, NORAD initiated some kind of weaponized EMP that was floating around somewhere in space on one of our satellites." He twirled his finger in the air as if pointing to the satellite while he talked.

"I don't know too much about the EMP, but what I do know is that it shut down the entire western hemisphere west of the Nevada border and as far as Hawaii, and as far north and south as Canada and Mexico. This only slowed the process for a little while on their end; but in turn it rendered our efforts fruitless for the time being. Command had us waiting on the Nevada border for a couple days before we got the all clear to head to the coast and start picking off the downed pilots that the EMP had grounded rather abruptly. The only thing we did not anticipate was the invasion of Alaska, Washington, Oregon, and California almost simultaneously. Everything has slowed to a snail's pace at this time, and we have been given the assignment to stop the pilots from speeding it back up. Reports are coming in about an armada of ships floating several hundred miles off the coast that are immobile since the EMP. However, once they get moving again we are going to be in a world of hurt." He leaned over to type something on the computer that was bolted down next to him on the center console before continuing with his story.

"I have also heard reports of refugee camps being set up on the Nevada, Idaho, and Arizona borders in efforts to prepare for the massive civilian influx soon to take place once everyone else realizes what's going on. They are also being established as a sort of permanent front in an effort to halt any possible advancing troops from moving farther east than the coastal states. I think the Brass are wanting to nip this shit in the bud as soon as possible before it gets way out of hand. It's only a matter of time before the dust settles and people start seeing foreign soldiers on our soil, marching down Main Street. When that happens the real shit is going to hit the fan. What's funny though is that they chose the West Coast over, say, the Canadian or Mexican borders to attack. My guess is that they watched, over time, the gun laws becoming more and more strict. So much so that any firearm a citizen might own would be more or less a laughing joke compared to what their soldiers would possess when they started their campaign. Who really knows, right? Either way we play this, a lot of people are going to die, and even more are going to suffer. This is turning into a really bad situation for everyone."

I felt like this whole conversation we were having was more or less him just venting off some overdue stress. Meanwhile, his volume level was starting to give me a headache since he felt it necessary to yell over the outside world. I think he failed to realize that our headsets enabled us to hear him quite clearly; either that or he just liked to yell. I did not imagine someone could reach his rank in his particular field without finding joy in the various levels of voice volume. I remember one of my brothers, at one time, talking about the excess noise their drill instructors would exhibit. They all seemed to find enjoyment in making sure everyone within a one-mile radius heard their voices. One time my brother said he was sleeping and had a dream where one of his instructors was yet again barking orders at him. The dream woke him with a start and he leapt out of bed and came to attention standing alone in the dark, his fellow recruits sleeping soundly around him in their bunks. To this day he still believes no one saw him, yet years later after the incident I met one of his friends from boot camp who asked me if my brother had told me the story about his nightmares yet.

I reached up to fiddle with the headset's volume control, wincing as I did, trying to minimize his effectiveness on the newly forming headache I had. Phoebe had seemed to check out, watching the landscape roll by as our little convoy headed north. Looking over my shoulder, I surmised that we must have already gone several miles since we started driving. The road looked clear ahead and a town could be seen off in the distance to our right, while the hillside continued towards the ocean on our left.

Stevens was still talking and I realized he was beginning to hit certain points that I had questions about, so I reengaged the conversation. "I have no idea how many enemy aircraft entered our airspace, but there seems to be a heavy congregation of special-forces units on the ground in the area. A few of the aircraft are smaller, one-manned operations, however, there were several larger craft carrying heavy payloads and a small group of Chinese, North Korean, and Iranian special forces units. The aircraft that were not completely destroyed in the EMP were able to dump their crews before they crashed into the surrounding landscape. The group we put down back there," he said with a gesture of his thumb pointing behind him," was one of several dozen that survived the EMP, yet were not dropped off close enough to their prescribed destinations and were scrapped for time, making due with what they had on their backs."

He paused and turned around to look at me. "James, we have reports of only a few of the groups getting to their rendezvous points to re-arm and re-equip. But we are at a key juncture right now; none of them have transportation due to the EMP. A few of them, like the last group, will figure out how to fix cars they find in the area; until then, they will all be like sitting ducks, just waiting for us." As he moved to face forward once more the humvee in front of us exploded. "Holy shit!" Stevens yelled, ordering his gunner to find the targets and return fire and demanding evasive action from the remaining drivers over the radio. Our humvee veered off the road to the right, heading for the open field that spanned for several miles until it butted up to the houses on the town's outer edge off in the distance.

"Thomas?! Move your squad to the left; the fire has got to be coming from those buildings in the northeast. We will head east, then bank north. Let's pinch these suckers!" Time speed up momentarily and the gunner confirmed Stevens' assumption of where the attack was coming from as he opened fire on one of the buildings off in the distance. We were not more than a hundred yards from the buildings when our gunner opened fire. The driver called out, asking for cover fire out the driver side, as we banked to the right before cutting back.

Stevens looked back at me and glared, "Get on it, James, use what God gave you dammit!" I lifted the gun off the floor and brought it up to the window. As I pressed the butt of the rifle against my shoulder, I searched for targets. This wasn't easy, the ground was bumpy, the sun was now low in the sky making my vision grainy, and there weren't any targets to be seen. "It's called suppressing fire, James, for Christ's sake, shoot, doesn't matter where, just don't hit our guys." I picked a building in the distance I knew I could hit and began ripping off three-round bursts. I watched as the paint began to chip off and a window shattered. The incoming fire did not cease, yet seemed to increase.

Something warm and wet trickled down my neck and I heard Phoebe cry out for help. I looked back at her and witnessed the gunner slumping down on top of her, the force of the humvee banking to the left causing his lifeless body to drape over her. Phoebe was struggling desperately to push the dead body into the back compartment area behind the back seats, but with no avail. His armor and sheer weight was too much for just her. As

I leaned over to help her Stevens hit me on the shoulder. "Forget him for now, nothing we can do. Get up there and man the gun, I need that gun running, James. Move, don't make me get up there, I've got bigger shit on my plate right now to deal with. Move, James, get your ass up there!"

I looked over at Phoebe and could feel myself smiling ear to ear. No way, I thought, this was going to be like every video game I had ever played. With one adrenaline-filled movement I pushed the deceased gunner into the compartment area and began my ascent to the main gun. My head cleared the hole first, branching forth into a whirlwind of air, bullets, and complete mayhem. The humvee hit a rut, sending dirt and grass flying over the roof of the passenger compartment. This caused me to lurch forward and strike my chin on the butt of the machine gun, and in turn brought me instantly back from a video game fantasy world where my head was going and into the stark reality that was this shit pile in which we had found ourselves.

As I steadied myself I could now easily see the enemy targets, at least a dozen lone individuals moving about in front of the buildings we were fast approaching. These buildings looked like a storage unit facility with no outside fencing. There was a small dirt barrier though, perhaps four feet tall that surrounded the facility, which looked to protect it from possible floodwaters coming from the valley we were in. The barrier lay about thirty feet or so from the buildings, and as we gained ground the enemy soldiers could be seen retreating the distance between the mound and the buildings in groups of three, leaving a few to cover them.

The soldiers out in the open became my targets, and I pulled back on the trigger. The gun heaved and let loose an amazing array of fire that obliterated the building just beyond the targets. My first burst missed everything I was aiming at, yet gave me a good understanding of the gun's capability. I took a single long deep breath and watch everything slow down as I exhaled. The second time I pulled the trigger I aimed at the remaining troops laying down suppressing fire and hit home, hard. If it wasn't for the intermittent tracer rounds in the available ammunition it would have been much more difficult for me to know where I was shooting. Out of the corner of my eye I could see the other humvee coming in fast on our left, bringing with it an almost glowing bolt of lighting spitting from the mounted gun as the gunner opened up and didn't hold anything back. The tracer rounds made our streams look like continuous bolts of electricity whipping about, which left behind devastating results. The incoming fire ceased as the final remaining enemy soldier, laying down covering fire, erupted in a molten pile of flesh and carnage.

Our humvees breached the dirt barrier and came to rest in the distance between the dirt mounds and the nearest buildings. The enemy was close, but had retreated far enough into the group of buildings that our current position was safe for the time being. I could hear them yelling at each other in the distance, but just barely though, over the constant rumbling of the engines. The dust cloud created by our arrival made any vision beyond several dozen yards impossible, and chancing a shot down range would just be a waste of ammunition at this point, not to mention giving our position away on the other side of the cloud. Three soldiers exited the other hummer and went to work dragging one of their own to the edge of the nearest building. From the looks of it, he didn't look any better than our own original gunner. One of the three returned to their humvee to retrieve something, and as he approached the rear compartment the vehicle rocked sideways and then keeled over backwards onto him followed by a sizable fireball. The heat from the blast seared the left side of my face as I attempted to shield myself with my arm and the cab.

From the other side of the cloud I could hear weapons discharging once more and what appeared to be intermittent RPG fire. Two rockets blew past our position and into the field behind us. Stevens jumped out and ripped Phoebe from her seat heaving her to the building where the remaining Marines had positioned themselves. Meanwhile he glared up at me and nudged down-range, sarcastically asking me, "What the hell were you doing?" with just one look. The driver floored the gas and we lurched forward once more, sending rooster tails of dirt up in the air behind us. I aimed to where I thought the enemy might be, or rather should be, and opened up the gun. Tracer rounds disappeared into the dust cloud, and I panned the sites of the gun back and forth providing what I thought to be sufficient cover fire. Stevens thought differently and had one of his cronies remove me from the gun. The humvee came to a stop after only moving twenty feet or so, and one of the other marines came over, opened up my door, and tugged on my leg yelling something I couldn't hear. I dismounted from the truck and he piled in. I made my way over to Stevens, Phoebe, and the last remaining foot soldier while the only working humvee sped off around the corner and into the cloud with just two marines onboard. Our numbers were shrinking.

Stevens looked pissed, but not at me. He generally just looked disgruntled at the way things were turning out, and why shouldn't he be. This was not turning out to be as routine as he had hoped it would. "James, we need to flank these assholes to the east, the humvee is going to work on their western flank. Phoebe, you need to stay here with the wounded and I am going to borrow

James for a bit." She looked miserable. The two soldiers leaned up against the building on the ground were dead, and the last remaining marine with us, besides Stevens, was busy stripping the dead for ammo.

"I do not have time right now to discuss tactics; let's just get this done. I counted about twelve of them before they moved. Most of these buildings around us are storage units and do not have interior corridors. We can pie corners and cover each other; just don't get jittery and shoot me in the back, okay. They are trying to cover too much ground, and if we stay to the outer edge we can pin them inside. Just watch for crossfire from the humvee; I told them to have at it and they sure as hell will. Got it? I'm on point. Let's go!" Stevens turned and hurried off, his last marine fell in behind him remaining several paces behind his leader. I followed suit while the humvee sped off around the western corner building in the opposite direction of ours.

Phoebe squeezed my shoulder as I passed. "Please come back, James." I looked at her and remember thinking that she was the only anomaly in this dream of mine.

"I will" I replied.

We came to the edge of our first building and the two of them closed in together. Stevens backed up away from the wall and then slowly approached, angling himself outwards and sidestepping away from the wall smoothly. This method was the safest and most effective way to approach any corner, and in doing so one could make sure nothing was waiting for them on the other side. As he finished he whispered, "Clear," and the other marine charged forward to the next building. We repeated this process on three other buildings before making a left turn and heading north.

We continued north, passing at least four other buildings without any sign of trouble. In the meantime, yelling and gunfire could be heard off to our left and maybe a hundred yards away to the northwest. The marines were either making them pay heavily or getting their asses kicked, either way we would be close to the skirmish in a few seconds. The last and final, most northern building came up just before the whole street we were on took a left turn and headed west. Stevens was about to turn the corner when he was knocked flat on his ass by a retreating enemy soldier and his buddy. Stevens grabbed one of them while the other marine grabbed the second. The two foreign soldiers were dead before they hit the ground and not a shot was fired or a sound heard that would give away our position.

Stevens stood back up and continued forward. I took note that these soldiers did not wear the same uniform as Duyi; they looked different too, yet still Asian. The letters, DPRK, were sewn onto a patch on their chest just above their left pocket while their name appeared on their right chest. The marine in front of me must have noticed my quizzical look because he scoffed while saying, "Democratic People's Republic of Korean Scum. Suck a bag of dicks!" As we all turned the corner Stevens had us spread out a bit, putting about ten feet or so between each of us. He kept his rifle aimed forward at ready, as did both the other marine and I.

The fight was getting closer and the machine gunner could no longer be heard spouting off rounds from the humvee, yet English-speaking voices still were heard and they sounded pissed. Stevens had us stop by raising a fist while he peered around the next corner. He opened his fist raising four fingers and told us to hold in place. He pulled out a grenade and in one motion pulled the pin and tossed it around the comer. He receded back behind the corner and waited. I had never been around when a grenade went off before and the concussion from the blast alone could be felt deep within my chest. It almost felt as though someone reached in and shook my spine with both their hands and a firm grip.

Stevens called for us to join him as he breached the gap to the next building and pressed forward. As we ran to meet up with him I was able to catch a glimpse of the grenade's destruction.

Four enemy soldiers had positioned themselves behind a loading dock and were using it for cover. The loading dock served as the location to load and unload belongings into a multi-story portion of the storage facility. What appeared to be a service elevator shaft was close by the loading dock door and climbed the entire four stories of the building on the outer edge, leaving several feet at the top for the motor and cable system. The four soldiers had settled into the area the trucks would back into, leading down a small, sloped driveway. They were using the loading dock for cover as well as the gradual increasing cement wall on the outer edge of the truck ramp. It looked as though the grenade had landed on the truck ramp and rolled down the driveway, creeping up right behind them. The blast must have exploded outward as expected and then hit the cement wall and loading dock, angling the force upward. As a result of this, body parts big and small littered the driveway ramp, loading dock walls, and the elevator shaft walls. Not a sound could be heard from the bloody mess left behind after the explosion as we ran by.

The humvee's machine gun could be heard picking up again and blasting into the surrounding buildings. Stevens kept his focus forward but spoke back at us, "There are at least three more of these bastards out here somewhere. We should head up one more building and then head southwest. From the sound of it, the humvee either has us covered from the north or has been overtaken, and we can approach it from the southeast. Ready? Let's go."

As we turned to follow him the marine in front of me, whose name I never got, silently keeled over dropping to his knees and falling lifeless to the ground. Stevens was gone, moving on to the next building and hadn't realized what happened. When the marine hit the ground one of the subsequent rounds being shot at us hit me in the chest and launched me backwards. Sheering hot pain scorched through my body as the wind was knocked out of me. I hit the ground, landing flat on my ass and falling backwards. I had enough sense to grab my rifle and roll over, looking for cover nearby. There was none and Stevens by now knew what was going on as he looked back in my direction from the cover of the next building. He gestured for me to join him and I did my best to limp over to where he was before the rest of the incoming fire tore apart the lifeless marine. I crumbled at Steven's feet, leaning up against the concrete corner of the next building and groped at my chest, searching for leaking blood and room to breathe. Stevens, meanwhile, watched sadly as his friend continued getting shot to hell behind us.

My breath slowly returned amidst the constant noise of seemingly never-ending machine gun fire. The pain was intense and increased intermittently with each breath I took. The armor I was wearing did the job, represented by the now fragmented ceramic plate I had over the soft armor. It felt like broken dishware in a pillowcase as I adjusted the vest to allow for my chest to rise and fall a few times unhindered. Stevens tapped my shoulder and I looked up at him. The past few moments seemed to have aged him severely. The dust was settling into the contours of his face and sharpened the creases in the sunlight. He looked beaten down and tired, but I sensed there was no way he would tell me that.

"Seems we are all that's left James, and there is still work to be done. Those shots that got you and Horton I think came from the humvee since I can see no other shooter in the area. Either that gun is still ours or we need to take it back. Moreover, I need to see if my men are down in the field. I am going to backtrack to where I threw the frag and see if I can get a better view from there. I'd like you to continue on from here," he said, pointing forward in the direction we were headed, "And we can flank their position. Just give me about thirty seconds before you move, okay." He paused for a minute and extended his hand helping me rise to my feet. "It's been a pleasure, James, I honestly did not think you would last this long if the shit hit the fan like it has. Tell your brother hello for me if you make it out of this, and good luck with everything." With a smirk he slapped me on the shoulder and headed off.

"Good luck to you too, Stevens."

He replied back, "Semper Fi," as he rounded the corner and was gone.

I checked my magazine and made a mental note of the fact I had not fired a shot yet since I changed out my magazine when we exited the humvees. I tightened up my straps on my vest that came loose when I fell down and cinched down my hydration pack. I took a deep breath and winced in pain after realizing I had already forgotten the recent shooting incident. God, I thought, this has turned out to be one hell of a day. I brought my rifle up and moved forward, taking note that the row of buildings had ended and this upcoming corner was the last one. I edged up close to the corner and peered around quickly. In the split second I had looked, I was able to see one marine down next to the humvee and another one corralled into a corner near some run down RV's only thirty or so yards from that humvee. The gun was manned by a loan DPRK soldier while two other DPRK soldiers lay motionless in the street. From the looks of it, the enemy must have charged the humvee and once the gunner was down the driver fled for cover. Now, the machine gun had our driver pinned down, and he appeared to be wounded, if not already dead. Stevens was nowhere, yet more than likely I would never be able to see him from my current spot.

I decided to lay down where I was and pick the gunner off from here. If I charged him, there would be no cover between his position and mine. The best chance I had was to get a clean shot from my current location and pray I struck home before he could retaliate or notice I was here. Lowering myself to the ground, I scooted forward and in one motion brought my rifle around the corner and aimed. Forty yards doesn't seem like much until your life depends on it. The iron sights provided little in the world of comfort I had grown accustomed to with the red dot scope, but I had trained enough with them to know what I was doing. And, no wind also helps.

He never even knew I was there. I fired one shot and stifled an internal shrill when the bullet tore a hole in the side of his chest just under his right arm. He slumped over, bouncing his head off the rim of the hatch before disappearing inside the humvee. I was in no hurry to move forward just yet. I wanted to wait and see what happened. Stevens, however, was in a hurry and ran right up to the humvee, looked in, fired two shots with his rifle, then headed towards his fallen driver. As he passed by the humvee he threw me a thumbs-up and flashed a cheesy grin as he jumped over one of the dead DPRK soldiers in the street.

I remained in place, maintaining good cover for Stevens and keeping an eye on the cab where the recently shot DPRK gunner lay motionless inside.

Stevens knelt down beside his driver and then stood back up shaking his head at me. He then rotated around and headed for the humvee, rifle aimed forward and ready. He peered inside and then dropped his rifle and reached for the door handle. As he opened the door an object fell out onto the ground at Stevens' feet. Immediately he bent over, picked the object up and threw it over the RV's. The grenade he threw didn't make it far enough and exploded twenty feet or so from him, slamming him against the humvee before he wilted to the ground. I waited several seconds, fighting the urge to run to his side, and watched the area. After several painstaking seconds I decided now was as good a time as any to make my move. I stood slowly, gun still pointed downfield, and walked towards Stevens and the humvee, remaining along side the building as I approached. It had seemed like forever at this point since I had heard what silence sounded like. There wasn't even a birdsong or rustling in the nearby trees from wind to break the silence. Every ten feet or so I would stop and listen, making sure no one else was walking close by. Stevens could be heard grunting with each breath he took, and I watched as he struggled to sit up.

By the time I reached the humvee, I had passed two other DPRK soldiers on the ground, and one other marine, who were all dead. I peered inside the cab and watched for chest rise and fall from the man I shot; I saw none. "Stevens, you okay over there?" I called out and waited for him to respond as I kept an eye on the interior cab compartment.

"I'm hurt pretty bad, James. I feel like I might be leaking like a sieve and could use a hand." I let my rifle hang by my side and swung it behind me while I pulled my sidearm out.

"Alright, hang on a second, I will be right there." With my free hand I reached inside and shook the DPRK's leg, keeping my handgun trained on him. No response. I opened the door and grabbed the pant leg closest to me and with one motion pulled him from the compartment letting his body flop onto the ground, keeping my handgun aimed at him just in case he might be one of those good actor types. Once on the ground, I dragged him over to the other two DPRK soldiers and proceeded to put a bullet in the head of all three. So much for the next Academy Award for any of these guys, I concluded, noticing that none of them looked to be any older than I was. Once I was satisfied the area was clear, I hustled over to Stevens and knelt down next to him. His face was bloodied and shrapnel was everywhere, in his legs, arms, torso, face, and sticking out of his armor.

"I sure as hell don't feel very good right now. You mind getting me out of here?" He looked up at me and tried to focus through the blood that was clotting on his eyelids while forcing a makeshift smile.

"Sure thing man. Let me help you up and get you in the cab, okay?" I put an arm underneath his left shoulder and heaved him upwards, after a count of three from me and a painful roar from him. Once he was on his feet and leaning against the back portion of the cab, I was able to open the rear driver-side door and push him in.

As I did this he asked me favor. "James, can you promise me you will take care of my men down in the field? Please?" When he was all the way inside and sitting down I closed the door behind him.

"No worries, Stevens, I promise I will take care of them. You have my word." I then got in the driver's seat and turned the engine over. Satisfied the vehicle would move, I silently thanked God for the fact the vehicle still worked and I did not have to lug Stevens on my own power somewhere. I pulled a u-turn and headed back to where Phoebe hopefully still was.

The last building was coming up, and so far no one was in sight. I worried for a split second, thinking maybe something happened to her or she beat feet when we didn't return quickly enough. My fears were confirmed once the corner was rounded and she came into full view. She stood there, five feet or so from the two dead marines, and she was not alone. A single DPRK soldier stood behind her, his rifle raised and pointed at her head. He looked wounded and tolerated a lean while favoring his left leg, yet remained focused and deliberate. I brought the hummer to a skidding stop and felt my jaw drop. Frick, I cursed internally, we freaking missed one! Why can't we catch a break at all today, I asked myself?

"Out of the car! Now!" He bellowed in a thick Asian accent. He did not speak English like Duyi had with an obvious American edge. This fellow sounded straight off the boat. "On your knees girl; hands behind your head. You, in the car, get out and lay on the ground." Phoebe's face was stricken with tears as the streams paved pathways in the dust and dirt that had collected on her face since this morning. I slowly exited the vehicle and lowered my rifle to the ground by its sling. Stevens could be heard softly asking me what was going on and I told him to keep quiet.

Once my rifle hit the ground the DPRK soldier began to repeat his order for me to lay flat on the ground while raising his rifle to point in my direction. Before he could finish his sentence I heard a loud buzzing sound, like that of a fast incoming bumblebee, come from the direction of the field. Soon thereafter, following closely behind that loud sound was the visually vibrant display of the enemy soldiers head exploding from the lower jawline up. His remaining inert body was then thrown sideways towards the building to his right. He hit the concrete with such a sickening thud that I irrepressibly became nauseated. While trying to account for what had just happened I noticed a new baseball sized hole punched in the side of the building. Upon impact with the ground the dead soldier began to twitch and make incompressible gurgling and groaning sounds for several seconds. A second or two later I heard the sound of a rifle's shot crack through the air above me like the sound of a whip. The birds in the nearby field came alive and went to flight, signaling me the direction I needed to take cover from. I crouched down to retrieve my long gun and called out to Phoebe telling her to get behind the humvee while I moved forward to the dirt mounds. I knelt down and slowly peered over the dirt pile into the vast field to the south. The birds were circling overhead and causing a ruckus; the cracked whip still echoed off the surrounding hillside bouncing around and creating an audible mirage that hindered my confidence regarding its origin. From far out in the field I heard a familiar voice. "Friendly's coming out! Hold your fire, James! You copy?"

Unbelievable, maybe our luck was changing. I rose to my feet and lowered my rifle. "Yeah, I copy! All clear!" I shouted back in his direction. Could it really be him?

Off in the distance, maybe a hundred yards or so, a lone figure stood and began moving slowly through the grass. His full-bodied ghillie suit meshed well with his surroundings. His suit made it hard to see him amid the adaptations he always added every time his terrain changed. Several minutes lapsed as I watched him effortlessly move towards me. He appeared to have suffered little in the last few days and looked at home in our current predicament. I knew he was grinning underneath his camouflage, the way he always did when any of us brothers were around. He always looked as though he had the upper hand in any environment and loved every bit of it. He'd never let you know any of this, though, for he was the humblest guy I knew. In fact, you'd never know what he did for a job unless you asked him just like the rest of my brothers. His only mistress was that fifty caliber Barrett he had with him that seemed to never leave his side. He kept her slung in front of him as he approached. "How are you, little brother? You look like you have had better days." I looked up at him and for the first time felt exhausted from the past several days and was able to let my guard down for a few seconds. I felt he sensed that and as he slid down the dirt mound he motioned for us to head to the buildings. I walked over to the building's edge and sat down, resting against it and leaning my head back, my eyes averting from the bloody mess close by.

"It's good to see you, Chaz. I was beginning to wonder if I would see anyone ever again." I extended a hand and he took it.

"It's good to see you too bro," he replied. "I saw a couple white vans pull out of the front lot of this place a couple minutes ago and headed north on the main road. Did you see them at all? I couldn't make out any specific details."

As I looked up at him I shook my head, having not seen them myself, and then suddenly remembered Stevens in the Humvee. "Crap, can you give me a hand? I've got a wounded friend in the humvee." I stood up and started for the humvee.

"Does that thing still drive?" He asked, "If so, I'll hop in and we can drive it over to the second checkpoint and take care of him there."

I paused and looked at him. "No way, the checkpoint is that close?" I asked astonished.

He just looked at me blankly. "Um, yeah, it's several hundred feet away. Why else would I be here? I, too, need to resupply at times also. Okay, in that case, how about you hop in and I will drive."

He emphasized the "I" when he spoke and I just gave him a look and then motioned for Phoebe to get in front next to Chaz while I took the seat near Stevens. "Why, hello little lady, what's your name?" Chaz asked as Phoebe got in next to him and closed her door. His exaggerated cowboy-like twist to the words was unmistakable as he peered over at her from under his boony hat. The engine rolled over a few times before coming to life and Phoebe responded by saying just her name. "Well, Phoebe, hold on, this ride is going to be very, very, very short."

I glanced over at Stevens and he looked like a man that had seen more comfortable moments than this in his time yet he was still holding his own. Chaz rounded the nearest corner and came to a stop after driving past only a couple of buildings. I soon realized we were, in fact, at the second checkpoint when I started to recognize the layout. As I got out to unlock the door I could see the loading dock off in the distance and knew we still had work to do around here if we planned to rest tonight. As soon as I pushed the roll-up door open, Chaz brought the humvee inside, and I closed the door behind him. Maybe, I thought, the day turned out better than I could have hoped.

Chapter 9

. . . Second Chances . . .

Chaz got out of the humvee and met me at Stevens' door; together we were able to move the injured man inside into the sleeping area of the storage unit and onto one of the beds. Phoebe led the way, opening the door as we went and making sure there was a clear bed ready for him. The man grunted and groaned as we stood him up and undressed him down to his underwear. The armor release tab had been damaged during his recent adventures, and the whole vest Stevens wore needed to be taken apart piece by piece while he stood looking longingly at the bed inches away from him. Phoebe laid down a clean sheet on the bed, and we lowered him onto it. The man was covered in blood and most of it had already dried in place, clinging to his clothes as we pulled them off. Some of the shrapnel pieces came out easily; there were several, however, that would require some work in removing. Chaz grabbed the field surgical kit and medical box we had in the storage unit and prepped an area for him to work. He then handed me the localized-numbing agent after he had drawn it up into a syringe and told me to get to work numbing the areas where he would need to dig for the remaining shrapnel.

Our older brother Eddie had gone to great lengths in training everyone in our group with basic first aid. A few of our members, Chaz included, received more training than necessary during their time in the military. Some others, including myself, were just downright curious about the medical side of things, enough so that Eddie spent time with us individually, and because of this we grew to feel comfortable around such things. It is amazing really, just how clueless the general public is around medical situations. I, myself, was once included in this broad category. When it comes down to it the human body, in a basic sense, is no different than a working machine, in fact it is one. Certain things need to work so that other things can function, and when something is not operating properly there are certain tell-tail signs to alert the observer as to what exactly is wrong. The easiest way, at least for me, to have learned how the body worked was to learn how blood flowed and how food and water were processed. Once you have the pathways of metabolism memorized, the rest begins to make sense. Much like a car engine, understanding how fuel and oil are processed to make energy enables the observer to understand how its working and gives them the ability to fix problems as they arise or prevent them from happening.

Phoebe stood nearby watching intently as I moved from one spot to the next, starting at Stevens' head and working my way down. His eyes widened when he saw the needle, and I reassured him we were trying to help. "Forgive me, James, if I am hesitant to trust you with that grin on your face as you hold that needle."

Chaz turned to look at me, then over at Stevens before returning back to what he was doing. "Cut the crap, Stevens, you know as well as I do he is more than competent."

Stevens looked over at Chaz and then up at me. "Yeah, I know he is, but could you tell him to wipe the smile off his face; it's starting to freak me out."

Phoebe cut in while I continued, trying my best to stop smiling, even though I felt like I wasn't in the first place, "Would you like some water to drink, Stevens?" She held a cup in her outstretched hand and he reached up for it.

"That's all you get, Stevens," Chaz said. "Any more and it may interfere with what I am going to need to do. I don't know how serious your wounds are yet. When I am through you can have more." Chaz still hadn't finished what he was doing and his back was still facing me. I, however, had finished what I was doing and set the syringe on the nearby stand set up for the used medical equipment.

"Let the medication set in, Stevens. Lay back and relax for a bit, okay. When he starts working, if it still hurts too much, we ' can give you more," I said as I stood up and went to the sink to wash my hands.

Phoebe had found the food easily, since this checkpoint was set up identically to the first. She sat nearby at the table, eating, and I came over to join her. As I sat down next to her, she handed me one of the MRE meals she found and I dug in. "You haven't said much to me today, you doing okay?" I looked over at her hoping to get some kind of response but there was none. Man, I really could not figure this girl out. She still looked good, even after everything that had happened to us today. The streaks from her tears were no longer visible on her cheeks, yet a slight redness in her eyes still was.

She looked up at me from her food and smiled. "I'm okay, James. I am just thankful you have shown me so much kindness these past few days. You don't even know me and yet here we are."

A piece of ravioli was stuck on the bottom of my MRE entree and I worked to get it free. "And yet, here we are." I smiled as I freed the ravioli from its prison and looked up at her. "Once Chaz is finished with Stevens, I can assume he and I will be busy cleaning up the area around outside. We need to hide some of the bodies and bury the marines. Unless we get it all done tonight, most likely we may be here a couple of days. Would you mind staying with him?" I asked while pointing at Stevens. "Chaz and I will need to get started here soon on the things outside and he might need someone to talk with."

Phoebe nodded at me and just smiled. "Of course, I don't mind. Just let me know if I can help outside too." I told her I would and got up to go find the armory section of the storage unit. I passed by Chaz who was now working to remove the fragments of shrapnel in Stevens' face, arms, hands, and legs. In the back of the room, in one of the several lockers, I found what I was looking for, replacement ceramic armor plates. I pulled the release strap on my vest and ejected the broken plate. Once removed, I inspected the plate, looking for signs of full penetration and the expended round. There was a hole in the middle of the plate, and inside the plate was the round I was looking for. I couldn't believe what I was seeing, the armor actually worked, but because I knew it was a fifty caliber round from the mounted machine gun, I did not celebrate. The only reason the round didn't tear a whole the size of a softball through my torso was because it had to go through two buildings before hitting me. Granted, the vest stopped it from killing me, but I was still plain lucky, regardless of how prepared I had been. I didn't like being lucky, but I guess it is better than the other side of that option.

Once the new plate was put into place I reloaded all my magazines, starting with the handgun magazines I had accidently neglected at the first checkpoint. I inspected my rifle and felt satisfied enough that the cleaning could wait a little while longer. I changed my socks knowing full well that I would change everything else later tonight; for now though, I wanted dry feet and my boots didn't breathe that well. I found a tactical helmet in one of the lockers and grabbed it for later, setting it down on the ground with the rest of my gear. Chaz was finished with Stevens' face and right arm; he was now working on the left arm and only had a few spots on the legs after that. Phoebe motioned to me she was going to use the restroom, and I stepped aside so she could get by. "You mind giving me a hand with this, James? All I need is for you to start suturing the larger sites while the smaller ones can be steri-stripped later."

I grabbed his suture kit and got to work on the larger gash, clearly visible now after the cleaning on Stevens' forehead. As I brought the needle over, Stevens tensed up. "Relax, jees, you're starting to make me nervous. I've done this a bunch of times, trust me." The laceration on his forehead took no time at all, and once it was closed I covered it with some antibiotic cream and moved on to the remaining injured sites.

"I really appreciate this, guys, and the last thing I want to do is ask more of you, but . . ." Stevens trailed off once he made eye contact with Chaz.

"Don't worry, Stevens," Chaz said as he continued to suture, "James and I are going to go out and make sure your men are secure as soon as we are done with you. Just one thing at a time, okay?"

Stevens seemed to relax a bit after hearing that. "Thank, you guys . . . Thank you . . ." He closed his eyes and allowed his head to sink into the pillow. I finished up with my sutures and steri-stripped the rest of his wounds. Chaz got up and left the room. I heard one of the humvee doors open, and then shortly after that I heard it close. Chaz returned from the garage area and brought with him a small pouch. He knelt down beside Stevens and took his blood pressure.

Once he was satisfied his blood pressure was high enough and stable, he pulled a morphine vial out of the small pouch he retrieved from the humvee. "Stevens, this is going to help with the pain once the localized agent wears off and help you sleep. I'm sure you don't want to sleep right now, but you need to. We need to leave this place eventually and the faster you get better the faster we can do that. Phoebe is going to stay with you while James and I clear the area." Chaz pulled the cap off the vial and drew up the medication. After giving him only a quarter of the medication available, he handed him an MRE meal and said to eat before he became sleepy.

Phoebe had returned from the restroom and was standing behind us, watching Stevens eat. Chaz turned to her and she told him she would stay with him. Chaz handed her a different vial from the small pouch with an auto-injector attached to it and told her if Stevens stopped breathing to inject him with the new vial. He informed her briefly that it counteracted with the morphine and to give him the whole thing if he needed it before coming to get us herself. She appeared comfortable with her new responsibility so Chaz left her in charge. I told him I was ready and he asked for a few moments to get ready himself. Pulling off his ghillie suit near the back lockers, he exchanged his clothing for something similar to what I was wearing and returned moments later ready to go as well. He had also pulled out one of the AR-15s and loaded it while walking over to me. He took Stevens' blood pressure once more and gave him a repeated dose of the morphine before heading outside with me. After closing the dividing door behind on his way out, Chaz then caught up with me at the roll-up door. I unlocked and pulled the roll-up door open and was promptly hit with a gust of cold wind. "This may suck a little bit James, but we need to give these Marines proper treatment." Chaz brought his hand up to rest on my right shoulder while he said this. Meanwhile, I hadn't breached the doorway yet and still stood inside the compartment.

Squeezing my shoulder with his left hand he spoke while remaining behind me. "It's good to see you little bro, I'm glad you are alright."

I pulled my rifle up and nestled the butt of the gun on my right shoulder and leaned forward, pausing to reply. "It's good to see you too, Chaz. I'm glad you made it as well. Ready? I got left."

He released his hand from my shoulder and I could hear him raise his rifle up. Quietly he replied, "Ready, I got right. Go!" I moved forward and cut left the instant I cleared the doorway and aimed downrange, keeping close to the wall, yet maintaining a distance of at least six inches away from it. I assumed Chaz did the same in the opposite direction, pulling right as he breached the doorway. The wind had picked up considerably and dust could be seen whirling about between the buildings in the distance. The sky was dimming and soon nightfall would be upon us. I muffled an "all clear" statement and Chaz did the same. He backed up to me, and I moved forward while he maintained a visual of what was going on behind us during our advancement. I never liked being the point man, which is why I always put myself in the position to be the lead. As much as I disliked it, I would never get over that by running from it. I knew I needed to immerse myself in it in order to find comfort with it. Still, I did not like it at all, especially right now.

Coming up to the end of the building meant we were going to be exposed from the opposite side of the road, easy targets for someone waiting. Chaz knew this and came up to my right side, clearing the direction to my right while I pied the corner and cleared left. We proceeded across the intersection and over to the next building and repeated this process for the remaining row of buildings on our little street. When we came to the end of the row, we found the flipped humvee and several bodies strewn about. Chaz covered me while I checked the DPRK soldiers around the area, starting with the two closest to us. Every soldier's body that we came to, enemy or not, had obvious signs of death present; anywhere from exposed brain matter to lividity or rigormortis was evident. Even though I was saddened to see some of these young Marines down, I felt comfort in knowing they seemed to not suffer. Well, all of them except one seemed to not suffer. When we came to the flipped humvee, I was reminded of the Marine that had run back to grab something just as the vehicle had been turned over onto him, crushing him underneath. His left arm was exposed out from under the upside down truck, and on his arm was a patch signifying that he was a dog handler. At that same moment I could hear the soft whimpering from inside the cab.

I pulled out a flashlight from a holster on my belt and knelt to see inside the cab. The gunner's hole in the roof, where he would normally stand and shoot from, had allowed for the Marine to be half crushed by the humvee as it flipped. His torso, head, and right arm were angled into the cab and his remaining body parts were crushed underneath the roof. Inside the cab one of the saddest things I had ever seen sat on display. It looked as though he bled out slowly while his dog stayed by his side. As I panned the light back and forth the silhouette of a German shepherd could be seen, lying poised next to his master and panting softly, tongue hanging freely. "Chaz, come take a look at this."

He came over and knelt next to me as I handed him my light. "I thought as much, this should never have happened to these guys. Someone screwed up and sent them into the middle of the hornet's nest blind." He stood up, clicking my light off and handing it back to me. "These are Force Recon guys, most of them I didn't know, but I knew Stevens and I heard of this dog. There aren't many in the service and especially none as good as she is. If she is healthy, let's get her out and take her to Stevens. He might be able to help her adjust to the losses." He turned around, placing his back to me and looked off into the distance. "No one else is alive around here," he said looking out into the open field we had crossed this morning after the initial attack. "When I came in earlier and found you I had passed by the humvee on the road. No one survived that either. What a waste this all was." He paused for a few seconds before shrugging it off and turning around to face me. "There is no sense in going out there tonight all the way across that field. Lets get Kato out from under there and take her back to the unit. She can sit tight with Phoebe and Stevens while we clean up this mess."

It was not easy getting her out from inside the humvee. She persistently did not want to leave her master and laid there growling at either of us when we tried to get close. I am fairly confident she would have stayed till she died of thirst before leaving his side, forever protecting him. Maybe that is why he was the only dead soldier we found with the remnants of a smile left on his face. Chaz had the idea of summoning Phoebe to retrieve Kato, thinking it may be a girl thing and perhaps Kato would feel less threatened by another female. I went back for Phoebe and grabbed a rifle sling while I was at it to use as a leash. Phoebe was more than happy to assist, given the fact she was essentially alone in the storage unit since Stevens had passed out and was resting unhindered. Plus, it helped her to not worry about our wellbeing, sitting alone in the unit with no clue as to what was going on outside. I could see the almost tangible relief in her eyes when she found out we needed her help for something else besides babysitting.

"What's the dog's name?" she asked as we walked back to the crash site. I hadn't forgotten where we were, but she apparently had since she walked indifferently behind me while I walked with my gun raised and ready.

"Her name is Kato and we'd like to take her with us if she's okay, but we can't get a good look at her without getting her out from inside the cab. Think you can call her out to you and stay with her?" I asked. She didn't respond, she just stayed close behind as we approached and then asked me for the sling.

As she took it from me, Chaz approached with his hand held out to stop her. "Phoebe this is an attack dog, a working dog, and it won't respond like a normal dog will. It would be best if . . ."

She pushed his hand away and walked right over to the humvee and knelt down next to it calling out the dog's name. Before either of us could stop her, she crawled inside and disappeared into the darkness.

"Good girl, come on . . . Come on, that's it . . . Come on . . . There you go, good girl . . ." Shortly thereafter she emerged from the cab, and Kato followed close behind, her collar and harness obviously attached to the sling.

"Well, I'll be damned . . ." Chaz stood back scratching his head. "I was not expecting that at all . . ." He looked over at me and I just smiled. She really was full of surprises, I thought to myself.

The rest of the evening was uneventful. We lugged all the Marine bodies into the field and dug holes for each one, which took us well into the night. Kato was especially attentive when we removed her handler from the humvee. She kept a careful eye on both of us as we moved his body into place. Each Marine grave was marked and properly identified for later removal. The DPRK soldiers were piled into one of the empty storage units far away from ours. When we were finished, the door was promptly closed without any identifying marks, and neither of us thought twice about it. They were lucky to get what they got and not be left out in the sun to bloat and rot. By the time we were finished with the body removal, it was around three in the morning, and both of us were exhausted but not even close to finishing.

We both knew our ticket out of this place and to the BOL was the newly acquired humvee in the storage unit. We needed to outfit it, put fuel in it, and paint it before we could use it. All the pieces to do that were right here; they just needed to be gathered. We decided together that under the cover of darkness would be the best time to recon the burnt humvee on the road that sat some distance away from us. We had passed on the idea earlier but kept coming back to it, and now it was becoming a necessity for success. If anything at all, there would be unspent ammunition in the back storage compartment that might have survived the fire in the ammo cans. Otherwise, simple body removal was important, especially to Chaz, being a Marine himself. Going to sleep right about now seemed so much more enjoyable, but there was work to be done and it could not wait until morning. If need be, we could sleep in tomorrow; till then, however, we needed to get things in order and be better prepared for the journey still ahead of us.

The trek out to the humvee left little to the imagination. I must have stuck my foot in a dozen gopher holes along the way. I can just picture what a fiasco it would be to make a run for it in the dark across this field. I'd never make it in one piece, surely breaking an ankle along the way. The tall grass swayed in the breeze, and a few crickets could be heard off in the distance while the ones nearby halted their music as we passed. I could smell the carcasses smoldering since we were approaching from down wind. That is a smell someone will never forget once they know what it is.

The outline of the burnt vehicle against the clear starlit sky was intense. Seeing the moonlight sweep across the jagged edges left behind from the fire that scorched its way through and around the metal sent a chill down my spine. My only hope was that they did not suffer. The entire seating compartment was toast, leaving behind disfigured tires and a still glowing engine block. The rear compartment had its outer shell in spite of everything, and from the looks of it had its interior as well. The rear seats must have shielded the back area from the heat and stopped the fire's progress. There was no point in removing the bodies, though, because what little was left of them had melted into the surrounding metal framework. The only visible parts left of the soldiers were their helmets and armored vests, beyond that they had become one with the humvee and made it their final resting place.

Chaz took in the area as he approached and did not stop moving to look. He kept in motion the whole time, heading towards the back compartment hatch. It opened without difficulty and we found inside the last six remaining ammo cans full of fifty caliber ammunition. He started pulling them out and setting them on the ground, opening and inspecting each as he did. I took note that the cans were charred black on the outside, but had maintained their form, and did the job they were designed to do, protecting the ammo inside of them. There was nothing else of use in the humvee, so we divvied up the ammo equally and started heading back to the checkpoint. The ammo cans were anything but light, yet we managed to make it all the way back to the storage unit, only having to stop twice to rest. My arms felt like they were going to explode by the time we reached the unit, though, and we took a moment to relax and get something to drink before we continued scavenging. Phoebe could be seen walking Kato about the grounds, stopping every now and then to look up at the sky. Kato seemed to really like Phoebe and would every so often nudge her thigh as they walked, as though she were making sure Phoebe was still there walking next to her.

Chaz came back out of the storage unit after checking on Stevens and confirmed he was sleeping soundly. He stretched his neck from side to side and let his rifle hang from its sling for a few moments while he cracked his back as well. "Our humvee has three quarters of a tank of fuel, I just checked now, so fuel won't be necessarily an emergency just yet, but we should take a look any how and retrieve some of the fuel cans on the flipped humvee. We might want to look into their navigation unit and salvage whatever else we can from it. I noticed we have some matte black spray paint cans inside of the unit. We should expend those on the humvee tonight before we hit the sack so that it can dry over night." He finished by taking a swig from his canteen and then wiped his mouth while looking over at me. I knew he was sporting that stupid grin he always has, even if it was too dark to see his face; I always knew, I could just feel it. "How are you doing by the way, little brother?"

Despite his grin I could tell he was being sincere. "I'm okay, I'd tell you if I felt otherwise, you know that. This whole, 'bugging out to our hide out' really isn't turning out like I had hoped it would. It's gotten out of hand almost entirely, and it's gotten really bad really quick. I always thought it would have a little more of a gradual onset, but not like this, not this suddenly."

"I agree, but it is what it is, and we are doing the best we can given the situation we are in and the way it's unfolding. In my opinion, you've done an incredible job with the cards you've been dealt this past week. Just think where you would have been if we DIDN'T decide to do this as a family? We all would have been so screwed and most likely dead. Which reminds me, once we are done with the fuel cans, let's check the receiver unit inside the checkpoint. If anyone checked in, I'd like to see who did and speculate where they might be right now. I'd also like to hear about what you've been up to the past few days. Sound good?"

I looked back in the direction of the flipped humvee and could see Phoebe making her way back to us from a few buildings over. "Yeah, it would be nice to sit and relax for a little bit. Let's get this done so we can."

We didn't find much in the way of supplies in the last remaining humvee. The only things available were several more ammo cans, some MRE's which we didn't need but wouldn't leave behind, and the two fuel cans still strapped to the side that had remained unscathed. We had already stripped the bodies before burial and found several letters home we would hold onto and return when the time was right and the means to do so were available. Besides the letters, there were only smaller amounts of what the humvees had. Stevens was right, this was a rushed mission, and in turn they weren't heavily supplied. What a waste.

Phoebe had now made her way over to us and stood nearby, Kato sitting silently by her side. "You boys almost done with what it is you're doing? Is there anything I can do to help?"

I looked over at her and said she could carry a couple of the ammo cans back to the storage unit, which she did without hesitation. Chaz and I soon followed suit, and we all made our way back to the checkpoint. While Phoebe and Chaz headed inside with Kato to check on Stevens, I pulled the humvee out and began to load it up. Everything still worked inside and had taken little in the way of damage during yesterday's firefight. A couple holes in the rear passenger side door were present, but beyond that we had found ourselves an exceptional vehicle.

Chaz returned outside, carrying an armful of spray paint cans and handing me a few. He took one side while I invested my focus on the other, taking one section at a time. Several paint cans later we had before us one entire, matte black humvee with a mounted fifty caliber machine gun, several thousand rounds of ammunition, enough fuel to get us where we needed to go and then some. Stevens had been tinkering with the onboard computer when we first met, showing me the location of the next insurgent group we were headed for; I wanted to take a look at that computer but would do so later. I pulled out several cases of food and water and placed them in the back of the humvee. After the events over the past few days, I wasn't taking any more chances on making it to the BOL in just one day. When I was finished loading the rig, I felt that the paint had had enough time to dry and could be parked inside once more without off-gassing too much throughout the night. Plus, we could close the interior door if need be. Once parked, I climbed out and shut the roll-up door and felt a wave of relief come over me; I could finally rest.

Chaz was inside kneeling next to the bed and attending to Stevens when I came in, and he gestured towards the receiver-unit with a head nod and a smile. I must have had a quizzical look on my face because he replied by telling me he would be right there, he just needed to medicate Stevens once more. As I passed by, Stevens looked up at me through doped up eyes and just said, "Thank you." Not needing to say anything more, he fell back to sleep and remained so till we would leave later that morning. Phoebe sat at the table getting some food ready for Kato and didn't seem to notice I came in. There was a long printed piece of paper that hung off the receiving unit and coiled up on the ground at my feet when I got over to it. I bent down and picked it up, realizing as I did that it was several feet long. "I haven't looked at it yet James, but by the size of it there's got to be some good news in there somewhere."

He almost sounded as excited as he had gotten the night before Christmas when we were kids. The highlights were there in the first five transmissions, the rest were icing on the cake. I read them aloud.

Eddie, 50 miles away CP2,

Drive, walk,

GHB, SA, Parents, 2W, 3W,

1-5 days BOL,

BOL

Dylan, at BOL

Total count present 42 at BOL

Covered

Howard, 125 miles away CP 2,

drive, walk,

GHB, SA, 4 extra members

1-5 days CP 2,

CP 2, BOL

James, 205 miles away CP 1,

drive, walk,

GHB, SA,

1-5 days CP 1,

CP 2, BOL

Chaz, 315 miles away CP 1,

drive, walk,

GHB, SA,

1-5 days CP 1,

CP 2, BOL

And the list kept going. From the looks of it, all of our family were at the BOL waiting for us, along with several dozen other friends and family. We were the only stragglers. A huge weight was lifted from my shoulders as the thought settled that everything we had worked for was playing out the way we had hoped it would. I looked over at Chaz, "You were over three hundred miles away from the first checkpoint? How in the heck did you get this far and this quickly?"

He just smiled at me. "Don't worry about it. I'm very resourceful." He winked at me, and I punched him in the shoulder.

"Don't wink at me, you dick. Seriously, how did you do it?" I knew once I asked the second time because the answer was becoming very evident. "You haven't slept since the attacks, have you? Jees, Chaz, I will never understand how you do that and still function the way you do." I returned my gaze to the piece of paper, "Hey, what's Eddies transmission mean?"

He sighed and looked at the printed piece of paper in my hand. His eyes watered and he looked over at me. "It means he has my wife and Dylan's wife with him along with our parents. That's my favorite transmission on here. Eddie really came through there; I can't wait to thank him for it. I wonder who else made it up there?"

Phoebe startled me a little when she began to speak right behind us. "Whatcha guys doin over here?"

Chaz tore the paper off the receiver and handed it to her. "This is the way we decided to let each other know where we were and what we were up to in case things went really bad. We all figured we could send at least one text before the cell-phone towers were overloaded in an incident. We set up this receiver for just that reason." He scanned through it quickly and then looked at me. "You know, the only one I don't see in here that should be is Travis's. The rest of the main team is in here, at least for the most part, I mean there are a couple missing on here, but I would have thought he might at least have transmitted something." I looked over at Stevens and caught a glimpse of Kato finishing her food and hopping up into his bed to curl up next to him.

I scanned through the printout as Phoebe held it. Chaz was right, despite Travis being a moron he still followed most of the rules. "I think I may know what happened to Travis, but I won't venture to guess just yet. Once we get to the BOL those suspicions might be confirmed. Look at this, though," I said pointing to Dylan's transmission. "From the looks of it, Dylan appears to have been in the middle of one of his weekend retreats up at the BOL with some of the members. How lucky are they, huh? What are the odds they would be up there when this stuff started to happen?"

He took the paper back from Phoebe when she handed it to him, and he began tearing it into sizeable lengths that he could post on the wall above the receiver-unit. "Yeah, no kidding, what are the odds? Come to think of it, I have a bone to pick with Travis too, as well, when we see him next anyways. He fell through on something I asked him to do a few months back and I've heard nothing from it since." He finished tacking down the printout on the wall and then turned to face me. "Oh well, let's get some rest, shall we? Kato can keep watch so all of us can sleep. I got dibs on top-bunk!" He pushed past me playfully and leaped onto one of the four top-bunks and pretty much fell asleep before his head hit the pillow. How in the heck does he just turn off and on like that, I wondered? It's not fair!

I went over to the sink and brushed my teeth and washed my face. I would eat in the morning; I was too tired right now. Phoebe hugged me again as I walked across the room, catching me off guard. "Thank you, James, I can't tell you enough how thankful I am for everything. I just want you to know that." She squeezed me hard and then let go.

"You're welcome, Phoebe. I haven't really done anything, but you are welcome, and you really only have to tell me once, it's okay." She smiled at me and then got into one of the lower bunks. I did a quick loop around the rooms to make sure everything was locked up tight and safe, realizing at the same time it was just past five in the morning. I then chose the top-bunk above Phoebe's bed and turned out the lights. I too was asleep before my head felt the pillow. I remember dreaming very little that night, having one of the best night's sleep I'd ever had. Tomorrow will be tough, but we will be ready for it.

Chapter 10

. . . For Those Whom We Love . . .

The sound of a gun being worked on woke me from sleep. I momentarily forgot where I was and stifled the panic that was desperately trying to breach my internal walls. I sat up and looked around. No light from the outside was able to get in, and the only visible light was coming from the table lamp nearby as Chaz sat bent over, working on his rifle. He didn't even turn around to face me when he spoke. "Good morning, little brother. How'd you sleep?" He pulled the slide back and forth several times, working in some oil he had just applied.

"What time is it?" I rubbed my eyes and was amazed at how refreshed I felt. Sliding my legs off the edge, I let myself fall off the bunk, landing awkwardly on the ground. As I balanced myself with my hands on the bed Kato just looked at me as she rested her head on the blankets, seemingly uninterested in what was going on around her. Her eyes shifted back and forth around the room each time one of us made a sound. Stevens snored quietly in his bunk, blankets held tightly up to his chin. Phoebe appeared to have squeezed herself into the crack between the bunk and the wall, attempting to inadvertently make herself seem invisible.

"It's about nine in the morning; we were asleep for just over four hours. Felt like more than that, so I'm not going to complain. Hungry?" He tossed me a bag of dehydrated eggs along with a hopeful glance at the cook-top.

"Ok, I will make us breakfast." I punched him as I walked past; the man never likes cooking for himself but loves to eat.

About halfway through making breakfast, the remaining two still sleeping began to rouse a bit. I threw on a pot of coffee and brought out some fresh canned fruit. "Come and get it. Stevens, I will bring you some but you need to get up and try to move about a little before we leave. We may need you today." He was sitting up now and asked where someone might go to use the bathroom. Phoebe pointed to the small toilet in the back and he sauntered over to it using the beds for support.

When he came out he came over to join us at the small table. As he passed by his bed Kato licked his hand. He jumped back, startled, and looked down at his bed as he grabbed his hand. "Kato! Oh, how are you girl? Come here!" Kato leapt from the bed and jumped up at him as he knelt down to greet her. "Where did you guys find her? This is amazing!" He and Kato played around the small sleeping area for a bit before he came over to join us, and we brought him up to speed. Kato sat right in the middle of

Phoebe and Stevens, looking back and forth between the two of them as they ate.

Stevens was both stunned and appreciative of what we did the night before. He was unable to recall the night's events and Chaz equated that to the medication he was given. "Chaz, you know as well as I do how much this means to me, but I can't begin to thank you enough." All of us ate feverishly, acting as though we hadn't eaten in days, and for some of us, that was true. I put a couple cans of tuna in a bowl for Kato, which she had eaten in seconds, and now sat appearing still as hungry as she had been before she ate.

"So what are your plans, Stevens?" Chaz asked, not wasting any time getting to the point.

Stevens looked up from his nearly empty plate and glanced at both Chaz and me individually sitting across from him. He took a drink of coffee and then sat back in his chair. "Well, what can I do? I have no transportation, no communications, no crew, and no way of knowing what else we are up against. And to top it off, I am sure my superiors think I am dead." He took another drink of his coffee while seeming to ponder his current situation.

"Well, there is the computer in your humvee Stevens, think that can be of any use?" I pointed in the direction of the other room as I mentioned it.

"That computer only has real time satellite mapping capability and acts as an intelligence gathering tool. I can't receive any two-way communication on it, we use our radios for that. So, unless you can find an undamaged radio, I'm out of luck entirely." He leaned forward, resting his forearms on the table's edge. "I know what you're thinking, what good is a linked computer if we can't communicate back and forth? It was one of the early designs and was never upgraded. Our regular vehicles are back in Southern California. We had to use the older model units. Like I said before, this was a mediocre plan at best that was set up quickly and botched entirely."

Chaz leaned forward again and repeated his question, "So, again then, Stevens; what's your plan?"

Stevens seemed to disappear within his own head for a few moments before coming to a decision. "Let me check something on the computer first and see if the satellite is back up and running. It went down a couple days ago and they told us they were working on it."

He got up from the table and staggered for a second. "Whoa, it's going to take a few tries for me to get the hang of that today." He opened up the door and was blasted with the smell of fresh new paint. "Whoa, going to have to get used to that as well, nice job fellas, looks brand new and you can't even notice the bullet holes." I sensed the sarcasm that was soaking up the room along with the paint fumes. After opening the passenger door, he got in and turned the computer on. A few moments passed, and then it came to life and he began searching. Chaz got up to go see what he was doing and I started cleaning. Phoebe got up and helped me while Kato followed her around the room.

"You sure you really want to do this, Stevens?" I heard Chaz asking him. "It may be best to leave this question unanswered for now until you can know for sure."

Stevens didn't respond right away, and when he did, he cursed and punched the dashboard. After we were finished cleaning, I headed over to see what the two other guys were up to. "Looks like I am going with you guys, if I can. Where can I get some fresh clothes?" Chaz pointed him in the right direction and then called me over to look at something on the computer. As Stevens passed by me on my way over to Chaz I noticed he had acquired an obvious limp after yesterday's ordeals. He picked up on what it was I was looking at and waved his hand in the air saying he was fine, dismissing the limp.

Chaz started talking before I arrived, "Stevens punched in the town he and his wife live in and more precisely his personal address. Look at what he found."

On the computer screen was focused satellite imagery of what appeared to be battle-ridden landscape in some Southern Californian town that I did not recognize. They all looked the same to me in any picture I saw. We had to use thermal imaging to see through some areas covered by smoke, but the general idea was evident, those areas were non-existent any more. From the looks of it, no nuclear explosion had gone off, nor had any large-scale bombings taken place. But, whatever had started the wildfire had allowed it to decimate the topography. Nothing survived its path, and the path was absolutely massive. Chaz fiddled with the computer a little and the view panned out, and a bigger picture reflected much of the same, there was nothing left.

"You are going to have to show me how to do that, but what does this mean?" I asked looking at Chaz who was walking away from the computer and me.

"It means we are going to have one more joining us for the time being," said Chaz. Stevens stood in the corner of the room, outfitting himself from our equipment stash and still favoring one leg over the other. He had already repaired and donned his body armor as well. Chaz was now doing the same, putting on his ghillie suit and loading his Barrett and sidearm while Phoebe looked over at me inquiringly.

"Guess we are leaving soon, Phoebe, you all ready to go?" I asked smiling.

Soon enough I stood in the empty doorway that divided the two units once again and turned out the lights as I closed the door behind me, having made sure everything else was turned off as well. Chaz sat in the driver's seat while Stevens called shotgun. I hopped in back with Phoebe, and Kato took the rear compartment, or what space was left over, after all the ammo and food was accounted for. If we came upon any trouble, Chaz told me to take the fifty-cal and eliminate any threats, but for the time being I could remain seated. The tactical helmet I grabbed from one of the lockers sat next to me on the seat. I felt better about having it, knowing that most everyone was already at the BOL and would not be needing it at this point. If anyone truly needed it now, it was I.

Flies had begun to settle on the drying blood found in spots sporadically throughout the storage unit complex. As we drove through, the flies would swirl about into the air only to quickly settle back down as we finished passing by. A large semi truck currently blocked the front gate, and the recent EMP gave us little hope in being able to move it without a tow. We opted for exiting the same way we had come in, through the field out back. As we rounded the last corner, Stevens asked Chaz if he could stop for a minute when the field came into view. Chaz and I had cleared a square area of soil the night before and placed all the Marines in a large mass grave with crude individual crosses for each. It wasn't much, but what more could two guys accomplish in a night that could do the job? Stevens stepped out of the rig and walked in front of the bumper, dragging his hand across the hood as he headed off into the field. "Give him a moment, he'll be fine." Chaz leaned on his left elbow, setting it on the open windowsill and left his outstretched right arm to cling effortlessly onto the steering wheel as he watched Stevens.

The man seemed to age yet again before me, standing in the sunlight atop one of the adjacent dirt mounds that surrounded the storage unit facility. He looked down at the small patch of freshly overturned dirt, and the minutes passed by without discomfort. Life had taken its toll on him during the last week, and if it was any other man I think it would have ruined him. Very few exist that can handle a whole world of shit being thrown at them and not despair because of it. To walk away unscathed is to walk away free, free to be the man you want to be and to seek the things you desire without restraint. Letting those against you win on the outside is one thing, but letting them win on the inside is another thing altogether.

We must have sat there for ten minutes or so, Chaz having killed the engine in an attempt to not drown out Stevens' muffled prayers. He walked from one cross to the next and paused at each long enough to pay each man his respect. It dawned on me as we sat there the absolute stillness in the air that was ever present and persistent. Without any running cars around, the world seemed to shut off completely. There were plenty of roads nearby, yet they remained entirely empty, bare of any sort of travel. We were going to draw a lot of attention, and I can assume the majority will be of the unwanted kind.

Stevens returned his hat to his head and came back to find his seat in the cab. He and Chaz said nothing as the humvee lurched forward, heading for the road in the near distance. I pulled the map book out of my front vest pocket and handed it up to Stevens who took it from me. "This is a list of several routes we can take, each one is color-coordinated to signify the distance and time it will take for that specific route. I recommend the Red Route since it is the shortest one on there that uses the least amount of freeway access. Plus, it also avoids the two major cities between our current location and the BOL." He scanned over it quickly then started working on the computer next to him. He brought up my mapped course on his on-board maps and compared the two in silence.

"Yeah, I don't think the Red Route will be the best way entirely, we may need to combine a few routes in order to actually make it there." He turned the computer to face me and pointed out what he was seeing. It didn't take much to understand the point he was trying to make. About ten miles or so before the fork, where the Blue Route split off of the Red Route on my map page, laid the remains of a small town and what looked to be a large-scale mobilization of some sorts. "I don't recognize a lot of what I'm seeing, but those sure as hell aren't American troops. We may need to steer clear of what's going on there for now. Hey Chaz, once you get on this main road here, head north for about thirty miles and then we'll take a westerly route for several miles. Sound good?"

Chaz banked the humvee to the left and brought the vehicle back onto the road, leaving the field and soft shoulder behind. I looked back over my left side and could see the burnt humvee fading into the distance, still sitting in the middle of the roadway. "Call the shots, Stevens, you're in the hot seat; I trust you. As long as you stick to that map James gave you, we won't have any issues. That map is all we'll need to get there."

Phoebe reached up and tapped Stevens on the shoulder, "You mind if I take a look at the map for a few minutes?"

He handed it back to her, "Be my guest."

Chaz took up the entire road as he placed the painted centerlines on the asphalt in the middle of the hummer. No one was on the road, so there's no sense in obeying the rules, I thought; we need all the space we can get right now. "Stay alert guys, I can't watch everything, so I need all the eyes helping out." Chaz looked in the rear view mirror and made eye contact with me as he spoke. I nodded at him and he returned his eyes to the road ahead of him. For the next couple of hours, things were very uneventful. Stevens kept up his part by guiding Chaz along the preplanned routes, and Phoebe and I kept busy watching the area as we passed by. A few people opened their front doors, having heard us approach and kept a watchful eye on us as we passed. But, for the most part, we kept out of large populated areas and were able to concentrate our time spent driving to areas less inhabited by anything more than a couple farmhouses. Things didn't become difficult until we came to an area on the map that was unavoidable. The last and final city we would be forced to go through lay sixty miles south of the BOL and was densely populated. Last I heard, it housed around twenty thousand people on any given day.

Stevens saw this coming earlier in the day and had asked Chaz to stop a few miles outside of town so we could figure out what to do as a group. There were several options, there were always several options to any problem, and people just tend to ignore them when emotions are involved. Chaz pulled the humvee off onto a dirt road that had a grove of trees on either side about three or four miles outside of town and killed the engine. Again, we were thrust into a world of absolute silence. A few birds could be heard in the distance, but the absence of engine noise was incredibly mind numbing. I couldn't see a house or structure for miles in any direction, but we had rules and the second we break them people get hurt for no good reason.

"We need to clear the area, Stevens." Chaz said as he opened his door and grabbed his Barrett from the roof where he had strapped it on one of the rails.

"Copy that, I got your six." Stevens exited and moved to the rear of the vehicle.

I got out and moved to the front. Chaz headed for one of the nearby grove of trees and found cover next to one. While crouching down, he surveyed the area through his scope, and Stevens and I did what we could with regular 20/20 vision.

Meanwhile, Phoebe waited in the cab. Soon thereafter we confirmed everything was clear and Phoebe got out and brought Kato with her. Both of them needed a break, as did the rest of us. "I can hear you guys from here, so talk it over and I will chime in if need be. Someone needs to maintain watch at all times." Chaz did not look at us as he spoke, knowing full well he didn't need to teach us anything we already knew.

Stevens unfolded the map entirely and placed it on the hood while I headed over to meet him, letting my rifle hang under my right arm as I walked. "Look at this. If I'm seeing this correctly, there's a road just up ahead that intertwines through the farm fields and primarily stays to the outer edges of the town. Does that look right to you?"

I leaned in as he spoke to get a better look at what he was talking about. He was right, there was a road but it encircled the town, yet was unpaved. "Yeah, that could work, it's a dirt road, though, but we won't have any issues there with this," I said as I tapped the hood with my hand. The road being unpaved is the reason we did not highlight it as a preplanned route to the BOL. Not everyone driving to the BOL in our team would have vehicles capable of taking the dirt road, so we chose to pick routes most easily accessible to all parties. However, just because it wasn't chosen did not mean we couldn't take a look.

I looked over at Phoebe after seeing her out the corner of my eye. "How're things, Phoebe?"

She was pacing about, and periodically Kato would pause to smell the area or pee. Looking over at me, she responded, "I'm good, Kato is good to go as well whenever you are ready."

I looked over at Chaz while Stevens was penciling in some markers on the map. "Ready to go, Chaz?"

He turned around to face me this time, "Always," was his reply. Before getting back in, I pulled one of the fuel cans off of its latch on the outer rear compartment and headed to the fuel tank opening. "We are at about a half a tank so put the whole thing in, that will more than cover us for the rest of the way and then some," Chaz said as he walked towards us. I unscrewed the cap on the canister and gave Chaz a "thumbs-up" as he secured his Barrett and got back in the driver's seat. While I was refueling, Phoebe returned and had Kato hop in first before she followed closely behind, getting back into her seat as well.

Stevens had his compass out and was finalizing some last minute thoughts down on paper before he to got back into his seat. He punched in our coordinates and received some real-time imaging of the road we were soon going to take. "Everything looks good from the sky. There are a couple houses out there but nothing more than we have already seen today."

I finished emptying the fuel can completely, and then returned it to the latch on the outer shell of the cab. "Sounds good to me," I replied, "Let's get going, yeah?"

Chaz slapped the side door and chimed in, "Yeah, let's go, old man; quit taking so long back there." I got in my seat, and before

I could get into position on the machine gun Chaz stopped me. "Not right now, James, I'd rather not draw any more attention to us than this humvee already does. If something happens, get on that gun as fast as you can, but otherwise, hang tight down here with us, okay?" It sounded good to me; being up on that gun gave me the willies, because I kept thinking some lucky bastard was going to take a shot at me and blow my head off without ever letting me see it coming.

I sat back down and buckled myself in. I peered over the seat and placed my hand out to say hi to Kato. She looked at me and then leaned in to be petted. "Good girl, Kato," I repeated several times over as I petted her head and scratched behind her ears.

"She is warming up to you, isn't she?" Phoebe stated more than asked as she smiled at me.

"Yeah, everyone does in time," I said with a smirk and she lightly punched my arm.

"Not everyone, James, just the right ones."

Chaz performed a quick three-point turn, and we were back on the road. Soon enough the turnoff came into view, and Stevens directed Chaz to take the dirt road to the left. As Chaz slowed to complete the transition from paved road to dirt, the smell of smoke and ash could be faintly smelled in the air around us. "Maybe it's a really good thing we opted out of heading into town." I looked out my window and concluded by saying the air didn't smell quite right and had a bad edgy feel to it. The cab fell silent and for the next few bumpy minutes no one really said much of anything. I think we all were mulling over what might be going on in that town we decided to bypass.

I had, over the passing months, hated when things slowed down; every time they did, I found myself and the thoughts I possessed wandering. Usually they wandered aimlessly, but more often than I would have liked, they headed towards her and the many reasons I concocted in my head for why she left me behind. Oh, how I wish I could think of other things, and how I longed to be free of her at the same time! For the longest time I would try to fight these thoughts and the graves they dug for me on my own, but as time progressed I learned to cry out to God for help, begging Him to rid me of my internal anguish. I think the mere request for help was enough at times. Just the act of figuratively reaching out beyond myself to be rescued put a new twist on things, changing the game ever so slightly. However, I do feel He assisted me in ways I may never fully understand, because in those trying times I did feel my heart calming like rough waters after the passing of a storm.

I must have looked troubled while I sat in my seat because Phoebe reached out and touched my shoulder while I stared out the window away from her. "You okay, James?" I looked over at her and could tell her words were sincere. "Who ever you're thinking about, I'm sure they are alright." She squeezed my shoulder and smiled before going back to looking out her window. My own struggles had kept me from seeing the beauty all around me for a long time. For some reason, Phoebe just looked breathtaking in the afternoon sunlight. Her outline against the bright backdrop of the low horizon behind her was stark and vivid. I wonder how many other sights had gone unseen by me since this darkness settled in my heart. I had stopped talking with God for quite some time now, having let the world beat me to a pulp and, for the time being, win. Maybe Phoebe was my wake-up call, to show me the world was indeed a good place still, despite all the hatred within my own heart for it.

A bump in the road jolted me back to reality, and Chaz held up a hand in apology for his bad driving. "One of the first houses is coming up around the next bend in the road; there wont be another one for several miles and then we have the turn off to the BOL shortly after. Keep an eye out, guys, I don't want someone to surprise us as we pass by." Stevens said all this as he was looking over the map folded in his lap. "Copy" was all anyone said in return from various places throughout the cab. The only person more skittish than someone living in a populated area was someone living in a rural area. In past situations the rural inhabitants were the ones that suffered the most under the hands of highway bandits and thieves. Because of the rural setting, help couldn't arrive for quite some time, if ever, making them easy targets for malicious crimes and acts of violence. As a result, farmers and rural inhabitants tended to be trigger happy and quick to protect what was theirs, and if they weren't, they didn't last very long because of it.

We rounded the bend in the road and the farmhouse came into view; it was set back from the road several hundred feet with a long driveway leading up to it. The house was backed up to a low hillside, and the main portion of their land was spread out on either side of it. A simple livestock fence surrounded the property, and brush could be seen growing around the outer edge of the fence in all directions. The house appeared quite quaint, with two stories and a surrounding porch. Just next to the house sat a large garage-like barn with one big door in front and a typical hayloft door above it. The structures were quickly coming into full view as we were coming up to them. Just as we passed the driveway, Stevens requested that Chaz immediately stop so that he could look at something. Chaz did so, and then backed up to the edge of the fence-line before it broke off and headed up to the house along the driveway.

Stevens stepped out of the rig, pointing to the puddle on the ground next to the paved roadway in front of the dirt driveway leading to the house. "There are wet tire tracks leading to the house from the road, multiple ones. I haven't seen any running cars in a while, except for the ones the DPRK and Chinese special-forces units were working on the day I picked up James." Chaz strained to see what Stevens was now referring to; meanwhile I was looking past Stevens at the dark farmhouse in the distance. Everything looked deserted, unused for quite some time. Except for the tire tracks, nothing else looked like it had been touched in a while, save for a few leaves bustling about in the quiet wind. Stevens shut his door and said he wanted to take a closer look.

Chaz looked back at me and tapped my knee, "Time to get up on that gun, buddy . . ." He was cut off as our humvee rocked to one side violently. I looked over at Stevens and everything began to slow down dramatically. Chaz's voice became distant as he started to curse and fumble with his seatbelt. Phoebe opened her door in time to catch Stevens as he went down, lowering him to the ground.

I disregarded the machine gun, jumped out my door and ran around the back of the humvee to help get Stevens back inside so we could leave. As I was rounding the edge of the hummer

I could see muzzle flashes from the upstairs windows in the house, as well as several individuals coming out and standing on the porch pointing at us. I raised my rifle and took a few shots at the windows, hoping it would be enough to halt their fire for a few seconds, giving me enough time to move Stevens. I came around the passenger side to find Phoebe struggling with the weight of Stevens on her leg. He was unable to move but looked more scared than I had ever seen someone. "Me legs don't work, James! My damn legs are gone!! Shit! Help me up please, help me!" Kato began to bark relentlessly inside the humvee, and at the same moment our machine gun came to life. Chaz had gotten out of his seatbelt, and instead of coming around to help us he jumped up on the gun and let loose on the farmhouse.

I remember when I was a kid I got my first booster shot before I went off to school, and the resulting pain was unparalleled to me at that time. The bullet that tore into my left shoulder as I was attempting to lift Stevens hurt far worse than anything I had ever felt up to this moment. It crumbled me and slammed me into the humvee. At the same time, a shower of expended fifty-caliber casings began to pour down upon us from on top of the humvee. Over the thunder of the machine gun Chaz was bellowing at me to get my ass in gear and get us out of here. I knew full well he wouldn't last long on a mounted machine gun that was stationary. He was all they were trying to shoot at this moment. "Come on, Phoebe, push!" With all my might I hoisted Stevens up and flung him head first into the rear passenger seat. Phoebe ran around to the other side and pulled him in. As soon as his legs were inside, I slammed the door shut and flew into the driver's seat. Slamming the gear into drive, I floored the gas pedal. The wheels spun and kicked up an amazing cloud behind us before we cleared the dirt and returned to the paved road.

I looked over my shoulder at the farmhouse and could see several DPRK uniformed soldiers running towards the barn. My heart was in my throat. "They are coming for us, James, keep going. You know the rest of the way, right?"

I leaned my head so I could yell up to him in response. "Yeah I do, I got this. Phoebe, how are we doing?" In the rear view mirror her facial expression said it all, we were screwed.

"Damnit! Oh no, no damnit! I can't feel my legs, James! They punched a hole in my gut as big as my fist; I am so messed up!" Stevens was thrashing about while holding his abdominal area with both hands. A bloody mess oozed out from under his hands, and I told Phoebe to put something on his wound. She found a shirt back near Kato and placed it in his hands. Kato was leaning over the back seat and licking Stevens' face, trying to do the best she could to help. He was right though; we all were screwed right now. If these people followed us we might accidently lead them to the BOL, and that would put everyone in jeopardy. The machine gun let loose again, raining more expended ammunition down upon Phoebe and Stevens while Phoebe cradled him in her arms. Things were bad and getting worse by the second.

My arm ached, but I could still use it for the most part. Gripping the steering wheel was becoming more and more difficult with my left hand, but I could manage for now. I examined my wound and noticed minimal blood loss; it could be ignored for the time being. A bend in the road was coming up, and if I remembered correctly Stevens mentioned that there were a couple of other houses before we reached the fork in the road that would meet up eventually with the main road to the BOL. If we could make it to the fork, perhaps we could lose them there. The bend in the road came and went; in the distance I could see a couple houses off to my right that edged a hillside and floored the gas pedal. The machine gun ceased and Chaz wiggled his way back down into the cab and up to the front passenger seat. "Keep it floored, James; give us some distance so I have enough time to get ready." I looked over at him while he was fidgeting with his pack that he must have grabbed from the back seat area before sitting down.

"Get ready for what?" I asked while I returned my focus to the road ahead of us.

"When we get to the fork in the road, I am going to get out and you are going to continue on without me. No questions, you got it? This is how it has to be." His attention was still focused on his bag, but I could tell he knew I did not like his idea at all.

The houses came and went, the intermittent trees along the sides of nearby fence-line rolled past, and the road behind us was clear still. I took some deep breaths and wondered if this was the last time I might ever see my brother. I looked over it him again and felt honored, filled with pride over the fact that he was my flesh and blood. We had grown up together and taken separate paths, but we would always be connected, through everything and anything. "Don't look at me like that. You make it seem like we will never hang out again." He projected that shitty grin of his in my direction, backed up by perfect teeth and a jaw-line that would put GI Joe to shame. "When I get out give me time to grab one of the fifty cal ammo boxes and my gun strapped to the roof. Once I am out, get moving. You have about ten miles left to the road leading to the BOL. Who knows, maybe the team will see you coming and lend a hand." I laughed a little at that; the likelihood of any of them wanting to blow their cover was null. I don't doubt the team cared for me, but there was a bigger picture here and it was entirely more important to not be found; even if it meant my suffering because of it.

Several minutes passed and the fork in the road began to rapidly present itself up ahead of us. Chaz reached back and grabbed one of Stevens' hands, who was now looking very pale and weak. "It's been a pleasure brother, I am sorry it played out this way. Do you have the letter?" What letter I thought?

Stevens reached into his left breast pocket with his free hand and pulled out a bloody white envelope. Meanwhile, Phoebe was now holding the towel on Stevens' abdomen and Kato sat with her head resting on the back seat watching this unfold. "Thank you, Chaz." Stevens said handing the envelope to him while they still held hands.

"I will find Vanessa if she is still alive and get this to her." Chaz focused on Stevens as he spoke, "I promise you that and know full well you would do the same for me. You take care, okay." With that they finished shaking hands, and I stopped the Humvee in the middle of the road just before the fork. Chaz exited the vehicle and slung his backpack on while closing the door. As he rounded the back edge of the hummer, he opened the back hatch and leaned in to pet Kato.

The dog licked him on the face as if saying goodbye while he pulled out a box of the fifty-cal ammunition we had stored there last evening. He closed the hatch and then came around to my side and set the box down on the ground. "You going to be alright?" I asked as he reached up to unlatch his Barrett from the rooftop.

"Am I going to be alright?" He laughed, "I am always alright you know that. Don't make what I am doing right now a waste though. You got that? Take care of them, James, like I know you can." He put out his hand, and I shook it with my one good arm. With his other free hand he pulled out a clean white envelope from his left breast pocket and handed it to me. "If you don't hear from me in a few weeks, give this to Michelle, okay? She'll know what to do."

I took the envelope, my hand slightly shaking, and looked up at him. "It was good to see you, Chaz, make sure it's not the last time I do, okay."

He smiled at me and winked, "Deal." He slung the rifle over his shoulder and picked up the box on the ground before turning around and hustling in the direction of the nearest hillside. We would be, very shortly, taking the left road of the fork and he was heading in the direction of the right side of the fork and the nearby rock outcroppings on one of the hills overlooking the area. From there he would make a stand and hopefully draw them in the opposite direction of where we were headed.

As I began to pull away a flash of fur shot in front of me over my lap and out my side window. Kato hit the ground running, and I slammed on the breaks screeching the tires. Chaz turned around and peered back at me, then down at Kato who stood between us at the moment, looking very confident in her decision. "Looks like she is coming with me instead, I'll look after her; will be nice to have the company anyways." He waved us on and turned back in the direction he was originally headed, whistling for Kato to catch up. The last time I saw him as we rounded the next bend he was trotting up the slope, Kato right on his heals appearing to be enjoying herself immensely. They were both in their element again.

Chapter 11

. . . Our Footsteps Are Heavy . . .

Once past the fork in the road we had about ten miles or so until we reached the last turnoff to the BOL, after which another couple of miles remained until we would reach the cabin on the property. I was hoping we could enter through one of the tunnels on the outskirts of the compound, cutting short our trip by a half-mile or so. In good weather, visibility from the lookout pits stationed around the BOL could be very good; allowing the viewer a clear line of sight a couple miles away. Maybe, they might be able to see us from there or if anyone was out scouting the area like we had planned. If they were watching, I wouldn't need to draw attention to myself because they would find me, and most likely they would find me well before I found them.

It felt wrong, leaving Chaz behind, but I reminded myself that he was now in his zone of comfort; on his own and being out numbered was what he lived for. I knew right about now he was setting up on that ridge, sighting in the area and getting ready to unleash fire from the heavens upon those poor bastards trying to take us out. They would never see it coming. All the while, he'd have that smile on his face like he always does. I sure hope I see him again soon.

Something popped outside the cab and shook the vehicle causing a low, humming noise to become a new constant addition to the rig. What was that I thought? I turned the steering wheel left to right slightly and noticed it was no longer responding as quickly to my adjustments. "That doesn't feel right, does it?" Phoebe asked from the back seat. I shook my head, still focused on the road ahead. The engine started to sputter as well, creating an ominous feel to the ride. I looked down at the gauges and saw that the fuel tank was bone dry. That isn't right, I filled it up earlier and had noticed it was around three quarters full when we dropped Chaz off. Something was wrong.

"I think we sprung a leak. Phoebe, and possibly blew a tire. I am going to pull us off the road as far as I can to take a look. Maybe I can put a temporary fix in place." The trees were beginning to thicken and multiply as our elevation grew. The closer we got to the BOL, the more trees we were finding. If I could pull the humvee off the road enough, maybe we could hide in the tree line and then, if worse comes to worse, we could walk the rest of the way.

"James," I looked in the mirror at Phoebe, and we made eye contact. I knew without her saying another word that Stevens was gone. He had become more and more quiet, moved less and less since we left Chaz behind. The wound he had suffered was a fatal one, given our situation and lack of help. He knew it, and the rest of us knew it. I just wish we were able to have said goodbye in a better way than this. I veered slightly to the left and let the humvee coast off the road and down a small embankment past a few trees. I applied the brake and turned the wheel, placing the rig behind a clump of trees, pretty much out of sight from anyone on the roadway.

I put it in park and got out. Now, because of the trees, everything was darker, despite the fact the sun was still high in the sky. The air was cooler also, and my breath was just barely visible amidst the backdrop of the growing forest around us. "Come on, Phoebe, help me get him out and set him on the ground." I opened her door and she stepped out, giving me space to reach in and drag his lifeless body out onto the ground. I pulled him over to one of the nearby trees and sat him up next to it, allowing him to lean on it for support. When I stood back up, Phoebe was standing next to me, both of us over Stevens' lifeless form on the ground, his head bent over as if he was taking a nap. Blood covered her stomach, hips, and thighs from having Stevens resting on her during the drive here. Her hands were crusted over with dried blood that stretched up to just below her elbows. She looked exhausted, and I felt it too. "I'm going to see what we can do to fix up the hummer; maybe it won't be as bad as it feels like it is. You okay?"

She nodded, not taking her eyes off Stevens. "Yeah, I'm okay. Can I help?"

In the distance, I could here the familiar sounds like that of a long whip cracking in the air. Over and over again the crackling noise would sound off. Soon one large and very loud explosion shook the ground, and I knew Chaz had his work cut out for him at that point. Whatever those DPRK soldiers had was bigger, louder, and possibly much deadlier than Chaz's fifty-cal. If I were unable to fix the hummer in a couple minutes, then we would need to start moving without it. Otherwise, any chance of escape might be gone sooner than I had originally thought. The crackling sound continued again followed by another larger ground shaking boom. "Phoebe, forget the hummer, prep your pack quickly, and bring only what you'll need for one night out here. If we hustle we can easily make our destination by nightfall." She snapped out of whatever trance she was in as she inspected her clothing and began preparing her backpack. I pulled mine out from the back hatch and swung it over my bad shoulder, letting it nestle into place and then tightened down the straps. I looped my rifle sling over my two shoulders and brought it to hang on my right side, as I inspected the magazine and made sure I had enough ammunition on me. When I was finished, I looked over at Phoebe who stood ready, waiting for my next move.

"Let's go that way," I said as I pointed northwest. "The road itself stretches out for another ten miles or so, but if we head this way on foot it's about half that distance as the crow flies." I looked over at Stevens, sitting peacefully against the tree, "We'll come back for him later and take care of the body then, he'd understand. Ready?"

She looked at him and then over to me, "Yeah, I'm ready."

I could hear her following close behind me as I turned and began heading into the thickening woods. I pulled out my compass initially and found my direction and mentally marked an object up ahead of us and aimed for it as I pushed my way around shrubbery and over fallen trees. Once I reached my first target, a solo tree, I aimed the compass and picked another target off in the distance. I would repeat this process for the next couple of miles as we continued on our northwestern direction. We soon ventured down into a valley, and the sounds of distant engines could be heard behind us somewhere. No telling if they were headed in our direction or away from us, for the time being I decided to pick up our pace and made sure Phoebe kept with me.

So much of what was going on now, I did not completely understand. I had so many questions, and the unanswered voids in this story had chipped away at my sanity over the past few days. Sure, the periods of slow, steady boredom interrupted by shorter periods of sheer and utter panic had clouded my ability to fully appreciate the situations we were facing. But now, as we trotted through a forest I had never been in to a facility that I had only pondered living in some day, all while being chased by unknown assailants for uncertain reasons; I was beginning to acknowledge our situation as dire.

The puzzle seemed to be fitting together, but some pieces were still missing, and finding them did not look to be an option at this point. Perhaps in time, if I ever saw any of it past today, the questions I had might be answered in a way I could understand. We soon cleared the small valley, and just as we hit the edge of the next tree line, one of the trees close by started spitting bark at us. A few pieces hit Phoebe in the face, causing her to bend over at the waist and clutch her eyes with both hands. She wasn't hurt, but the shock factor of it all scared her a bit and caught her off guard. As she was bent over I turned back to look at her and could see them. Six of them were coming out of the trees opposite us and a couple of them were already firing at us. The rest, well the rest were preparing to join the two already shooting at us as they raised their rifles and spread out into the field.

"Run!" I yelled as I reached out and grabbed the top strap of her backpack and yanked her forward. As I did this I spun around and brought my rifle up to aim in their direction. I started spouting off rounds as I backed into the tree line, not appearing to hit any of them. I turned around again to join Phoebe in her flight and noticed the bees had returned. The sound of bullets whizzing by had become an all too familiar sound now, and I did not like it any more now than I did the first day we experienced it. The sounds just reaffirmed the danger was way too close for comfort. Up ahead the tree line thinned again and broke free into another open valley, this one much larger than the last. Phoebe, now thirty yards or so ahead of me, was running faster than I had thought possible. When I stepped foot into this new valley, the immensity of it struck hard. We would never make it to the other side before they caught up with us. There was no cover out here! Why was I still running into it? I looked left and saw that the valley spread out as far as I could see, away from the tree lines and hillsides. I looked right and noticed a slow climbing grade to the base of a few rolling hills. At the base of these hills were scattered trees and large rock outcroppings. If we could make it to them we just might be able to find cover, enough to make a stand at least. From there, well, from there we might be able to find a better way across this valley. Maybe along the base of the hills around the valley would be our way to go, but for now, getting to those rocks was our only hope.

"Phoebe! Head to the right, up the hill to the rocks!" I yelled this as I banked right, hoping my voice could be heard over the thundering sound of her footsteps and the pounding heart in her chest. She knew as well as I did that we were in trouble. All we needed to do was get to those rocks; I could figure out the rest once we were there. Phoebe was making good time; I, however, was lagging behind her, and what made it more difficult were the growing pains in my feet from being on them for countless hours during the last few days. The bees returned and began nipping at the air around me. Phoebe's backpack exploded as the contents poured out of a newly placed hole in the back flap. She appeared uninjured or didn't notice anything and picked up speed. "Zigzag, Phoebe! Don't just run straight! Start moving around a little. Make it harder for them to hit you!" I struggled to get the words out in between breaths, desperately trying to maintain my breathing and footing simultaneously. The rocks were close, very close now. I caught up to Phoebe before we hit the outcroppings and did my best to motivate her.

Every step sent shockwaves through my body; the pain was becoming relentless and the agony of defeat crept up on me with each passing moment. I maintained my speed, running as fast as I could, zigzagging around rock outcroppings in the hillside and pressing forward with every desperate muscle I had left. Phoebe kept with me, matching my steps and gaining ever so slightly as she tried to get ahead of me. Her mouth was held tight in a fixed grimace, attempting to fill her lungs with each painful, deep breath she took. Seeing her, summoned strength within myself that I no longer thought was there. I had to survive, if not for myself then for her. Slow, unstoppable motion was all that I could comprehend while bullets struck the ground and rock all around me. They could be heard screaming past us, and soon enough they were felt ripping into me. My right thigh was hit first, crumbling my stature to the ground. I pushed up with my arms and was able to prop myself onto one knee before another round struck my left shoulder, for the second time sending me back to the floor. I cried out in agony as I rolled over onto my back, staring skyward, and gritting my teeth in pain. Explosions could be heard in the distance, and I feared they would soon be much closer. That ever familiar thumping sound of a grenade being launched is ominous.

I looked over at Phoebe who had also been hit. She lay several yards away nursing a wound while hiding behind a small boulder. The ground was shaking all around us as the concussions from the impacts were nearing themselves to our location. Soon thereafter, one of them hit home, sending both Phoebe and me into the air. We both hit hard as we returned to the ground, and Phoebe was knocked out cold. I rapidly performed a self-check, groping about to make sure I had all my limbs and everything was where it was supposed to be. My right hand reached up and felt the absence of flesh from the right side of my face; the vision in my right eye had worsened, and meanwhile a sizable amount of blood began to pool in the surrounding dirt.

Was I really dying?

I could see them now, advancing on us, moving swiftly through the field, approaching the outcroppings we had taken refuge in and raising their guns to fire upon us once more. Not like this, I thought, I will not go out like this, laying here like a beaten dog! I rose to a knee for a second time, shouldered my rifle, and pulled ever so delicately on the trigger as I aimed down range towards them. The kickback on my uninjured shoulder felt good, like coming home from a long extended vacation or enjoying the company of a good friend. I smiled as each projectile careened away from me, searching the world for someone to hurt. Some of my little children made contact, while others simply struck fear in the hearts of those that wanted us dead.

I looked over at Phoebe who was coming around and conveyed to me through one look that she would rather be anywhere else than here right now. The familiar explosions could be heard again, and I knew this time they would not be so forgiving. I smiled at her thinking that this day had started out too pleasantly to end like this. What a shame it would be to not see the sunrise with her tomorrow morning like we had been doing together lately. I crawled over to where she was and laid down next to her, holding her outstretched hand as she cradled my head upon her chest. While listening to the sound of her heartbeat I was overcome by the feeling of failure, that I had let her and the rest of my family down by not making it all the way to the BOL. With tears welling up in my eyes I begged her for forgiveness, feeling responsible for everything at that point. "I'm sorry, Phoebe, I didn't mean for it to end like this, to bring you all this way and have it end here."

I struggled to swallow, my mouth becoming very dry all of a sudden. She cradled my head in her lap and told me it was okay, that everything would be okay. I remember letting go at that point, feeling freed by her words and relaxing for the first time in several days. Then I thought out loud, "Oh well, at least we'll have this one last sunset together . . ."

Her words seemed to drift in the evening breeze, barely audible amidst the gunfire and fragmenting rock all around us. "It's alright, James, you have done well. Our Father is proud of you. You have shown a complete stranger kindness when no one else would and for that, I will be eternally grateful. The journey ahead of you is quite unfinished, because, my dear child, it has only begun. Rest now, for you have earned it. Let the angels I have sent to protect you do their job . . ." She stroked my hair and leaned in to kiss my forehead. As her lips touched my flesh the ground began to shake in anticipation of the next explosions, and I felt everything go dark as I slipped away into the vast lake of unconsciousness. My last thought was of her, and the words I had just heard, wondering what they meant, wondering if she was the one that actually said them. Perhaps, instead, someone had spoken them through her to me. I could still hear her as the darkness wrapped itself around me, drowning me within its warm embrace, "May He always watch over you and keep you safe . . ."

Chapter 12

... And Then There Was Only One ...

The room was dark, very dark, only a single light could be seen down a long and narrow hallway that was leading to the room. My eyes were adjusting as I attempted to open them; however, the vision in my right eye was still limited. Where was I? I tried to call out for help, yet was unable to do so. My throat was extremely dry and my voice sounded coarse, inaudible even to my own ears in this small room. I blinked my eyes a few times and tried to sit up. Pushing myself upward sent painful shockwaves down my arms, and I decided it might be better to take one thing at a time. Laying my head back on the pillow almost seemed like defeat in this dark, damp room. Yet, the pillow felt so good, softer than anything I had ever felt before. I ran my hand down the side of the bed and realized it too was also very soft and comfortable. I managed to find a little more comfort in the idea I was at least mustering some intent to get my vision under control and not just lay here apathetically. I realized my vision was partially shoddy because my eyes were almost sealed shut with dried blood and crusted mucus build-up. Using my good right arm, I reached up and rubbed my eyes. I forgot about the wound on my face and winced in pain as my hand brushed over it. Once my eyes were cleared as much as they could be I was able to notice the man in the doorway. His sudden presence caused me to jerk backwards in an unanticipated fashion; this resulted in more shockwaves of pain resonating throughout my body and a groan to emanate from my throat.

I wondered when he had gotten there, or if he had been there the whole time. I could only make out the stature of this man, for the rest of his features were hidden by the darkness that seemed to permeate every inch of this room and hallway. "Who's there?" I called out, "Where am I?" He took a step back into the hallway and extended his hand to reach one of the walls nearest him. The brightness of the one lonely light increased, as did several others that were previously off. The room now possessed an eerie glow, and this new feature allowed the lack of interior decorating to be seen. He dragged a chair from out in the hallway into the room and sat down, leaving several feet still between us. He leaned back in the chair and brought one of his legs up to rest on the other and took a sip of his coffee while he looked at me. I still could not make out the details of his face, which remained continuously shrouded in the shadows, but by now I had a good idea of who he was.

"You've been out for a few days now, there was one point we didn't think you would make it," he paused to take another drink of his coffee which by now I could smell and longed for my own. "Mom and dad were starting to worry until your fever subsided. I'm supposed to debrief you before you start getting up and moving around . . ."

I cut him off mid sentence by asking him a question I'd wanted to all along, "Where is she, Eddie?"

He looked at me and cocked his head to one side appearing perplexed by my train of thought. "Who? Mom? She is back at camp with dad, she is okay; why does that matter?"

I pushed myself up and swung my legs off the bed, ignoring the immensity of pain now being distributed throughout my nerves making them pulsate in agony. I leaned back and sank into the concrete wall that my bed was nestled up against. I reached over with my right arm and cradled my left. Ugh, would I ever feel any better than this again? "No, not mom, Eddie. Phoebe, where is she? Is she okay? What have you guys done with her?"

He leaned forward in his chair, arms resting on his knees, and held his cup in both hands. "I don't know who you're talking about, James, but hold on a second. I'll get Chris and see if he knows anything." The look of sincerity was obviously apparent on my brother's face, but he was in charge, how could he not know the answer already? Eddie got up from his chair and walked over to the doorway. He pressed a button on a small black box secured to the wall and then looked over at me. "No worries, little bro, we'll figure this all out."

The intercom rang back and an indifferent male voice could be heard on the other end that I did not recognize. "This is Com, go ahead."

Eddie leaned in and pressed the button when he talked. "Hey, this is Eddie, can you have Chris come to Forward Room 6; I need to talk with him." When we were not on the radios the lingo was less formal. The operator confirmed his request and said they would get right on it.

"Forward Room 6, huh. What, don't trust me?"

He smiled in my direction, "You know the drill, trust no one till they prove otherwise. You are just recovering here; once you feel up to it you will be welcomed in. That much is obvious to everyone." He walked over to a desk in the corner of the room with a water pitcher on it and poured a glass full. He then returned to his chair and handed it to me. "You look like you could use some." He was right, I really could. I snatched it from him and drank it all in seconds. By the time I was finished, he had retrieved the whole pitcher and was pouring me my second glass. "Chris is going to be a little while; why don't you fill me in on what's happened during our wait. Where have you been the last few weeks, James?"

One of the many things I liked about my brother is that he was the type of person who, if he asked you a question, expected an answer and offered up as much time as you needed to do so. He liked to talk; in fact one of his favorite things happened to be good conversation with friends and family. But, he didn't like to hear himself talk, to simply ask rhetorical questions all day long just so he could have the pleasure of his own company. No, not this man that sat in front of me now. This man expected an answer and was sitting patiently waiting for one. I looked down at the glass resting in my hand and finished it off before starting. What seemed like minutes were actually a couple of hours and soon enough I had him sitting on the edge of his seat in anticipation. I am not one to embellish any story I tell, but someone listening to me now would be hard pressed to not think I was. The last few days were a blur of insane coincidences and overwhelming odds that were almost entirely against me, yet I still seemed to have come out on top. I had finished up telling the last few bits and pieces having to do with the last day I remember, when Eddie stopped me mid-sentence after hearing the intercom beep.

"Just a second, James, I should check on this." He slid his chair back as he stood up and walked across the room towards the hallway. "Go ahead," he said speaking close to the intercom as he pressed the button down lightly.

"Chris is now getting back from his patrol; he has Conrad and Phillips with him and they would like to speak with James. Would that be possible?"

Eddie looked over at me and I nodded at him. "Yeah, that's fine, send them all down here. Have them bring some food as well." He walked back over to me once he was sure his request was processed. As he sat back down, he reaffirmed what I was saying about Phoebe. "So this gal was with you ever since you started your trek here? Nothing seemed unusual about her?" As he asked this I suddenly recalled Chaz.

"Hey, where's Chaz? Did he make it back?"

Eddie adjusted his position on the chair and waved a hand in the air as a gesture of dismissal. "James, you and I both know there is no point to worrying about Chaz. I'm sure he's fine and will pop up sooner or later." He was right. Our parents soon learned after Eddie's first few steps into the real world as the first born, and general guinea pig, that worrying about their kids would be inevitable, but losing sleep at night over our safety, now that was pointless. Boys will definitely be boys.

My family strongly believed that God was watching over us and would stop at nothing to protect us. As the years passed I lost that belief system as my own a little bit at a time, due to a constant barrage of worldly depression. The real kicker that thrust me over the edge of lost faith was my ex-girlfriend leaving me after having promised to never do that. Because of my already dwindling faith in God, my new lost faith in humanity, secondary to lost love, sent me over the edge. Soon enough that support structure I had been instilled with at such a young age, which had carried me for years, rotted away, leaving in its wake a relentless tidal wave of doubt and self-loathing. What seemed to happen next in my life became all too inevitable. The constant battles within my own head gave way to a serious lack of self-confidence, lost faith in family and friends, and an unbelievable lack of ambition. When Eddie came to me with a list of goals and a hope that I would join him, well, only then was I able to pull myself out of the muck I had been caught up in. The only problem with this motivation was that it had to be self-generated, and soon enough I would grow weary again.

I needed to restore my faith in God, in something higher than myself, but had neglected to do so these past couple of years. As a result, everything I had built this new life upon was being held up by my own inner strength. In time, it would surely crumble and I feared that it might do so in the form of a psychological meltdown. All the unfinished internal work, misrepresented passions, and unanswered questions would surely take their toll on my inner psyche, soon enough I might crack. Had I cracked now? Did I in some way make some of my story up to manage my stress?

Footsteps could be heard in the hallway. We would have company soon. Eddie reached out and tapped my knee, "Chaz is fine, or he took a hell of a lot of them with him on his way out. Just got to have faith, little brother. If you want these guys to leave once they get here, just say the word, okay? You still have some sleep to cash in." He stood up to greet Chris as he came into view. Chris had a tray with my dinner on it, which he set down on my bed before reaching out to shake my hand. We exchanged some hellos, and I asked how he was doing. I made sure before we moved forward in the conversation that I thanked him for finding me and bringing me back here.

Chris told me it was no big deal and then looked over at Eddie. "Phillips and Conrad are on their way; they'll be here in a few minutes. So what's this all about?" Eddie proceeded by asking Chris about the day they had found me out on patrol and, more specifically, if anyone else was with me.

Chris Shook his head in reply and then appeared as though he saw something very far away for a few seconds. "No, he wasn't with anyone," he looked over at me "We did find Captain Stevens' body near the humvee. Did we miss finding someone else you were with, James?" I nodded at him with a mouth stuffed full of green beans, and the two of them laughed at me. I smiled back, thinking I must be an odd sight and washed it down quickly with a third glass of water. I told Chris about Phoebe, leaving out most of the details.

"I will say this, we did see footprints in the hillside that weren't ours or yours, James. We had just chalked them up to them being from the DPRK soldiers we cleared out. It is possible that they could have been hers. They were smaller in size but, then again, those soldiers weren't much bigger than average."

Eddie peered over at me and shrugged as he said, "We'll look into it some more." He looked over at Chris and asked if he had anything else to add.

Chris shook his head and said goodbye, informing Eddie that he was off for the rest of the night and was going to head to bed. He would be in his bunk if anyone of us needed him further. "It's good to see you up and about, James; you had us worried there for a little while." We both thanked him as he left.

Conrad and Phillips passed Chris in the hallway as he departed and we could hear them talking for a few brief seconds before Phillips poked his head in the room and knocked on the door. "Hey, guys. Hey, James, how are you feeling?" Conrad came spilling in, never one for the formalities and walked right over to me and gave me a huge hug. Once he was finished he stood back and shook Eddie's hand, and Phillips came in the room after him. Both of them looked like they were about to explode with anticipation over what they had to say, but had waited patiently for the pleasantries to pass before saying any of it. "Okay guys, what's on your minds?" and with that, Eddie had opened the figurative door.

They proceeded to tell us about where they were when the attacks happened. From the sounds of it, they were a couple days behind me the whole way to the BOL. By the time the EMP hit, they were about a day's travel time, walking distance wise, from the first checkpoint. As a result of the loss of their vehicle, they had to walk the remainder of the way. By the time they reached the first checkpoint, they were exhausted and ready to crash. But, when they approached the storage unit, there were lights on inside and people talking. They told us that something didn't feel right the instant they heard the voices inside and decided to approach with caution. Armed only with their side arm handguns, they waited outside and listened. The voices coming from inside the unit sounded like two males, but were completely unrecognizable. They spoke in a way that was unfamiliar to Conrad and Phillips, using Spanish intermittently throughout their conversation. Just as the lights went off, they made their move. After a few moments Phillips stepped in as sole narrator, since the constant back and forth between the two was becoming difficult to follow.

"The door was not locked from the inside like it had been designed to be and slid up easily." Phillips shook his head and continued, "This was our final clue that these people did not belong in the storage unit. After raising the door silently only a foot and squeezing underneath, we posted up next to the internal entry door that lead to the next storage unit. When we bum rushed the room we came in with our flashlights out and our guns drawn, covering each other and ripping the two unwanted guests from their beds and slamming them to the floor. It was immediately apparent that neither of us knew who these men were nor what they were capable of. Conrad here," as he pointed at Conrad while he spoke, "in the confusion and thrashing about, accidently hit one of the males on the back of the head with his gun, rendering him unconscious. The second male lashed out at me with a recently unnoticed and unsheathed knife, and Conrad shot him point blank in the head. The sudden flash and sound from the blast in that confined space freaked the both of us out. We sat there for some time in the dark not saying a word, neither of us wanting to turn the lights on for fear of what we would see.

Reluctantly, I got up and flipped the lights on. The dead body on the ground wasn't half as bad as we must have envisioned it would have been. There was no mess on the wall or cranial explosion that took place. Instead, the man lay motionless on the ground, a small hole in the side of his head serving as a low flow faucet for a constant, oozing trickle of blood.

"We stood there looking at him for quite some time, neither of us knowing what to do. The last thirty years of our lifetime had been spent living in a society where law and order prevailed, or it was at least the assumption and desire for most. Now, suddenly, we had been spending the last few days in a world neither of us recognized nor were entirely sure how to act in it." Phillips looked over at me and his eyes narrowed, "So you know what we did, James?" I stopped chewing my food and looked at him, not really knowing what to say. He smiled and continued, "We buried the body next to where you buried Hector." I spit a little of the food out onto my plate in surprise, Eddie taking a step back as I did so that he could avoid the spray of green beans leaving my mouth. "Yeah, that's right, the unconscious bastard laying on the storage unit's floor told us about you and how Hector came after you with a fury of vengeance. Before getting rid of the body, we sat Jesse up in one of the chairs and tied him to it, making sure once he woke up he'd have nowhere to go. The only logical place to get rid of George, the dead guy on the floor, was too bury his ass out behind the buildings. When we got him over there, we noticed an obvious freshly dug up area of dirt in the shape of a gravesite with no markings. Eventually, we were able to put the story together after having made sure we didn't know the person recently buried in that unmarked grave. Which I might add was no fun digging up."

Phillips paused for a second and looked over at Conrad. "You want to tell the next portion?"

Conrad looked to be in deep thought, and after being prompted by Phillips stepped in and continued their story. "Well, like he was saying, Jesse spilled the beans on everything. Once we got back from our dig he was awake and willing to talk. Actually, he was more than willing to talk and almost begged us to not hurt him further, telling us it was all some guy named Hector's idea. Before we could even sit down and listen to his story, he began rambling into the details of it. This is where it got kind of scary for us, and for the rest of our people here at the BOL." Conrad took a minute and used the pause in the conversation to help emphasize the next portion of his story. "Travis never showed up here because these three guys killed him the night before the statewide attacks. Hector hatched some plan after Travis drunkenly told him about the checkpoints and the items we had stashed away here at the BOL. Travis brought on whatever hell he experienced before he passed, because from the sounds of it he didn't go quietly. There were originally five of them including Hector, and after the confrontation with Travis they lost a couple."

Conrad looked around the room at each of us and then continued, "So after Travis' place, Hector, George, and Jesse rounded up what they could and headed for the first checkpoint. Travis had done enough damage at this point with his mouth. Hector now had it in his head to pillage the two checkpoints, and then, if at all possible, head for the BOL and finish all of us off. I really don't think he knew what he was getting into to the full extent, but he could have done some real harm to all of us. Whatever the case may be, these guys were on the road for hours after Travis' place and more than likely they would have succeeded if the attacks didn't happen and put us all on alert. Honestly, if they weren't listening to the radio or had people calling them to tell them about the attacks, I am almost certain none of them knew about it. But, there was one thing along the way that they were certain of, and that was your truck, James." My facial expression must have been what made him stop talking for a few seconds. "Yeah, apparently one of Travis' social network profile pages had some pictures of you on it next to your truck, as well as some pictures around the BOL. There were even some pictures in his house with all of us at the BOL. Needless to say, your truck was in a lot of them, and let's face it, James, your truck is very recognizable."

We all stopped listening and laughed at that a little. He was right, my truck did draw attention before it was blown up and left on the side of the road. Conrad continued with his story and we all settled back down to listen. "So when they passed you on the road, they knew right away who you were. One thing led to another, and before you knew it they had set up an ambush with the hope that you would fall into it." He stopped talking to the room and focused in on me as he continued, "What they couldn't understand is how you knew they were waiting for you? You came around the corner, stopped well ahead of them, and drew your gun down on them. How did you know, James? How did you see that one coming?"

I looked at Eddie hoping to get some support after telling him my story already. He just looked at me in a way that told me this was my story, not his. "I didn't know, all I saw was a girl laying in the road and three guys running after her as if she had fallen out of their vehicle or perhaps they had hit her. That's what I thought at the time." Phillips and Conrad both looked confused so I tried to elaborate. "Look, there was this girl, Phoebe, and she was on all fours in the center of the road. When I came around the bend in the road she was just there, in the road, and these three guys gave me the willies running in her direction. So I stopped the truck, threw on my brights, and got out, drawing down on them for effect. I ordered her into my truck with the mindset that my company must be better than theirs, and we drove off together. I put a few rounds into their car to slow them down, but that was the last time I thought I would see any of them."

Conrad and Phillip stood up straight and looked at me, then at each other, and then back to me. "We never heard anything from them about a girl, James," Conrad said this with a concerned tone in his voice. "Jesse went as far as to say you seemed crazy, almost enraged, and he and George bolted for the trees."

I looked at them and then over to Eddie. "Come on guys, this is ridiculous. This has got to be some kind of joke."

Eddie's gaze narrowed with his reply. "You know us well enough, James, to know we wouldn't joke right now." He was right. We had talked about the reintegration of team members during an event such as this into the BOL and how it was not to be taken lightly. The debriefing I was going through at the moment was serious, something that would be recorded and documented. This was not a time to play any practical jokes.

"So, are you guys insinuating that Phoebe never existed or is some kind of figment of my imagination?" I was starting to get a little agitated and really didn't like where this conversation was going.

The room fell silent and Eddie slid his chair closer to the bed, "No, James, we aren't implying anything nor do we think you are lying in any way."

Conrad cut in like he tends to do at these kinds of times. "Look, James, we're just glad to have you back and really don't care all that much how that came to be. All we wanted was for everyone to get here safely, and so far that is turning out to be the case. But," he knelt down and put a hand on my knee, "if you ask me, this woman Phoebe sounds like she could have been your Guardian Angel. I'm just thankful you showed her compassion, like we have been instructed to do, and in a way we all can be proud of. Hell, I'd hate to know how she treated those who weren't kind towards her."

Eddie scoffed next to Conrad, "Well, we could ask Hector about that one, isn't that right, James."

Conrad and Phillips looked over at Eddie and then back at me. I shrugged and just smiled. "Damn, James reminded me to spend more time around you as this whole thing progresses. Seems like that is the safest place to be." We all laughed at that and Conrad and Phillips said their goodbyes, leaving Eddie and me alone once more in the room.

The sound of their footsteps disappeared down the long hallway and soon they were out of sight. The intercom chirped again and Eddie went over to check on it. What Com had to say this time sent a chill down my spine, "Hey, Eddie, we have a lone figure and a dog approaching from the southeast, they look to be about a mile out from the property line. He appears to be well armed. The patrol that's out right now is already headed to intercept him. Have any additional orders?"

Eddie smiled and looked over at me telling Com he had no additional orders and that we were headed their way. "Come on, little bro, there's still some work to be done." With that he walked over and extended a hand to help me up. Putting one arm under mine he helped me get situated on my feet, allowing me enough time to adjust to the new pains in my legs. Eventually we were headed for the hallway; Eddie seemingly able to effortlessly manage my weight along with his own. A faint smile could be seen at the corners of his mouth. My brother was clearly in his element and the confidence he had now regarding his current situation was very evident. "Looks like you'll have to rest up a little later, James. For now you can sit with Com and help them coordinate this patrol. I'm going to head out there personally and meet this newcomer for myself."

I looked over at him and smiled back. "Eh, no worries Eddie, I'm alright for now. It just feels really good to finally be home."

My Dearest Phoebe,

It has been some time since a day has gone by that I did not spend it thinking about you and our time together. As the days have grown in number I did my fair share of research and discovered that perhaps the name Phoebe was just something you chose so that I may understand, when in reality I should have been calling you by several other names. None of that matters to me, however, because of the simple fact that I am still here. Because of you and your intervening in my life I was able to survive a period of time where most likely I would not have otherwise. I lacked the courage, the strength, and the endurance to move forward during that time alone, and without you, I truly believe I would have never lasted as long as I did, and certainly not as long as I have so far. You may never read this or know how I feel, but I vow that others will. It is the others I am counting on to keep your story alive and to maintain with it a level of respect and gratitude in regards to the sacrifices you made for me.

I am able to sit now and watch the sunsets with my family, with the loved ones in my life, and with the people most important to me. It is with a heavy heart that I say I still sit here wishing you were with me by my side once more. I know it is because of the choices we made that I no longer have that luxury, yet a part of me feels it would have ended up this way anyhow, now matter how the dice was rolled. I do speak of feelings and emotions as if they are ours, but I know they are only mine and mine alone. If you are who I think you are, an angel sent to watch over me and protect me during my time of strife and struggle, then I know you are happy wherever you are. I pray for you every day, that God may be watching over you and keeping you under his mighty wing. There will always be a level of gratefulness in my heart for the time I spent sleeping safely under yours.

Rest well, Phoebe, wherever you are . . .

Forever,

James

For he will command his angels concerning you to guard you in all your ways . . .
-Psalm 91:11

Don't forget to show hospitality to strangers, for some who have done this have entertained angels without realizing it!
-Hebrews 13:2